PRAISE FOR P.D. SINGER

Fire on the Mountain —Rainbow Awards Jury's Choice Honorable Mention

"This was a well written, engrossing story and I can't wait to see where this series goes from here."
　—Pants Off Reviews

"…a sexy and fun and sweet story."
　—Under the Covers

Snow on the Mountain

"I highly recommend *Snow on the Mountain* to anyone who likes a romance mixed with misunderstanding, scandal, adventure, a little possessiveness, and a secret cabin in the mountains. It is as fun as it is sweet."
　—Joyfully Jay

"…another treat from Ms. Singer and I really enjoyed it."
　—Mrs. Condit Reads

Blood on the Mountain — Rainbow Awards Finalist, Honorable Mention (5*)

Read it for a cracking plot, and a wonderful couple that deserve their Happy Ever After.
　—Mrs. Condit Reads

Fire on the Mountain

P.D. SINGER

ROCKY RIDGE BOOKS

Fire on the Mountain
Copyright © 2020 by P.D. Singer
Cover Art by Cosmic Letterz

Print ISBN: 978-1-62622-084-3

First edition Torquere Press 2009
Second edition Dreamspinner Press 2012

Published 2020 3rd Edition

Rocky Ridge Books
Box 6922
Broomfield, CO 80021

For Eden, who shared the struggle,
and for Jo, who believed.

Fire on the Mountain

PROLOGUE

Flames danced on the dead branches low on the lodgepole pine's trunk.

"Damn it! I didn't think the tree would burn!" Kurt looked up from his shoveling to examine the tree at the edge of the woods. It had been smoking only moments ago.

"Stand back. I'll get it." I took hard swings at the tree's trunk with my long-handled axe, hacking away at the side farthest from the small blaze we'd spent the last few hours putting out. The chips flew with each bite of my blade. Some muscle in my lower back screamed in protest. Kurt kept a careful eye on my progress as he threw more dirt on the smoldering remains of the fire. "Better back off. I think it's ready to come down." I wasn't bothering to take the tree down neatly. Time was the bigger concern.

"Push!"

Kurt and I braced our heavy gloves against the bark and heaved, cracking the unchopped part of the trunk, toppling the thirty-foot-high pine to the ground, away from the other trees. It would not take its companions with it to a fiery end.

The tree crashed onto ground already scorched and disturbed, sending up a shower of sparks. We'd shoveled dirt onto burning mountain mahogany and grasses for half the day, trying to contain the fire before it went from heat and smoke to an open blaze. Between digging a firebreak and trying to deal with the burning material, it had been a busy few hours. The tree still bloomed with open flame; putting it out would mean the end of the hardest of the labor. A few minutes of brisk whacking took the crown of the tree off, letting us pull the unburned branches away from the danger zone.

The normally homey scent of flaming wood had a whole different meaning out here.

"So, rookie, what would you rather put out: a lightning fire or a human-caused fire?" Kurt retreated to the shade of the remaining pines to catch his breath.

"Whichever smolders more and burns less." I pulled off my helmet to wipe my forehead. The canteen at my side flapped loosely; I unscrewed the stopper and tipped it to my mouth anyway for the last few drops of water. We had more drinking water back in the truck, but I'd have to hike for it. Kurt took a long swig from his canteen and offered me the rest. The warm, tinny water tasted delicious.

We had left the medium-duty tanker on the one-lane service road that was the only sort of road through most of the Uncompahgre National Forest because we couldn't get it through the trees to the burn area. Half the forest stood miles from roads and had to be patrolled on horseback. The truck got left behind a lot anyway. We had to take what we needed from the equipment bins on the sides and do without the water if we had to hike too far back.

"Yeah, lucky you, that's lightning fires usually, and they outnumber human fires by a wide margin around here." Kurt waved me to follow him to some branches that were emitting puffs of smoke. "What do you think the score is?"

"Don't know." I threw shovelfuls of dirt at the felled tree alongside him. "The other five teams all had one or two fires each when we went into town last, and we haven't been called to respond to one of their blazes." I stomped a smoking branch with the heavy sole of my boot.

"And we haven't had to call anyone in for one of ours. Might be a tie, or we might be winning with three." He stepped back from the burn and unfastened his jacket. "The wind is down. Let's squirt a hundred gallons at it—it's out and it can damn well stay out." We gathered up the shovels and axes and dragged them back to the tanker. More often than not, we'd starve a fire into submission rather than extinguishing it with water in the dry, windy Rocky Mountains.

We'd caught this fire early, still in the "thinking about being a forest fire" stage. It was far enough from the road that trying to put it out with just the water we carried with us in the tank on the back of the truck was hopeless; until the wind dropped, we couldn't have shot it without losing three quarters of the spray. The loss wouldn't have mattered that much if we'd been close enough to a pond or stream to stick the intake nozzle in. Then we could have sucked the stream up and put it to good use without using up water we might need later that day. But no, the fire was far enough from the road and through the trees that we were lucky to have seen it at all, so we fought it the old fashioned way: with dirt, muscle, and cuss words.

Today we won. Losing a battle with fire out here could mean a hundred acres burned, or a thousand, and if it went really bad, it would be a disaster, like the Storm King fire. Fire-fighters had died battling that one, men and women who loved the wilderness and worked to protect it. I hadn't known any of them personally, but our boss and some of our co-workers had, and they still grieved. The mistakes that happened at Storm King got pounded into us to make us better rangers, to make us more effective firefighters. All this was new enough to me that the responsibility for the land weighed like a stone in my gut. I was glad not to be alone in the mountains for that and a lot of other reasons—Kurt and I made a good team.

Together we dragged the hose out to its full hundred fifty feet through the trees into a small clearing. Kurt jogged back to hit the pump, and I braced myself for the hose going stiff and ornery. The nozzle bucked in my hands as I struggled to aim the stream toward the fire; the water surging through the tube made it hard to control. I had to point it up and over the few trees between me and the burn site, making me glad we'd waited to do it until the wind died down. Kurt returned and steadied the hose from behind me. Four hands could accurately drop the water on the fire site, turning it from a potential disaster into soggy ash.

Together we pumped the water at the forest, and knowing my partner was behind me, helping me, made me feel just a little better. Fire was a scary thing, damned near alive but dangerous, mindless, and able to whup a lone man. The two of us, well, that was another matter today.

"Think that's about a hundred gallons, Kurt?" I'd been trying to estimate the flow just by time passing.

"Just about, Jake. Point it up," he suggested from behind me, "and hang on tight, I'm letting go."

Warned, I was ready for the jolt in the hose when he let go. I wasn't ready for him to sprint out into the private rainstorm I was making, but he'd left his heavy, fire-resistant clothing and helmet back at the truck when he'd gone to start the pump. Now he stood in dusty green utility pants and boots and nothing else, face up to the spray. The water came down on his upturned face, tilted to catch the arcing wetness, his mouth open and eyes closed, arms wide.

The droplets came down on him as he laughed and enjoyed the impromptu shower. The day was warm and the work had been hot, and now he turned from side to side to cool himself. Shallow rivers ran down his tightly muscled chest and arms and soaked his short, blond hair but couldn't make it lie down. Instead, the drops caught the sun, flashing the light back at me, and my breath suddenly came short.

The fire in the woods was out. But now there was a fire in me, and it was already raging out of control.

ONE

Fires would be part of my summer—I'd known that before ever getting up to the mountains.

I'd asked plenty of questions when I'd called the Chief. After a disastrous weekend excursion a little more caution was in order. A college seniors' last road trip that should have been nothing but fun had cost me a few friendships and strained some others, and there hadn't even been the consolation of an orgasm. The experience left me firmly in the closet, unsure about how to ever get out and wanting to get the hell away from people in general. Maybe a summer in the back-ass of beyond was exactly what I needed. Nobody to cuddle with, no one to fight with, no one to judge.

I'd work with one partner, possibly crusty and cranky, the Chief assured me when I finally called. And my new boss didn't seem to think I was overeducated or underqualified for the ranger service. I tested out of four classes, told the University of Colorado where to mail my diploma, and headed for the high country.

One partner with Davey Crockett skills and possibly nineteenth-century hygiene to match, I figured I could cope with. I hadn't figured on spending six months with the walking temptation named Kurt Carlson.

I'd driven my crudmobile Toyota, of a vintage older than my own, northwest on Highway 36 out of Boulder into the hills. Past mountainsides gone blue-gray with dead pines into the greener reaches of the high country, and hours later, I pulled into the tiny town of Meeker.

The bright balloons tied to the mailbox marked my destination, although the motley collection of pickups, SUVs, and a tanker parked in front of an unfenced, corner-lot brick house told me where the party was. I joined the group gathered around a picnic table and grill at the back of the house as instructed, to be greeted warmly by the Chief and again by Mrs. Chief, who directed me to a tub of iced pop cans.

The subdued chat among the group of mostly men didn't expand to include me; some of them clearly knew each other, and others might have been furniture for all they were saying. I tried introducing myself to a few of them and got grunts more than names. The crusty old mountain man, straight out of my imagination, ground my knuckles and grimaced something that might have been a smile from behind his bushy beard. He could have a whole family of deer mice nesting in there. I ground back best I could, but was glad to get my hand back with a few bones left unpulverized. The fire season suddenly looked a lot longer than six months.

It took me a few minutes to steel myself for another social attempt, this time on a tall, lanky man who looked more receptive to a conversation than the Sons of Grizzly Adams.

"I'm Rich," he told me.

"No, but you're cute," his female companion cracked and offered her hand to me. I took it carefully, which made her snicker. "I'm Abigail. Rich and I are partners. Have you met your partner yet?"

"I'm hoping it's not the guy who just tried to break my hand." I cast a backward glance at Old Crusty. At least these two were about my age and speaking complete words.

"Nah, he's on a horse patrol team. We won't see much of them unless we're all called to one fire." Rich chuckled, eyeing my attempts to realign my fingers. "I saw the assignments and think you'll be out with Kurt Carlson."

"That's more than I knew coming up here." I decided my hand might be usable again in half an hour or so. "You know him?" I glanced around the group, wondering if the mysterious Kurt was another knuckle crusher.

"Oh, sure! This will be our third fire season together. He's— well—" Abigail shut her mouth with a snap, and her squinched lips were doing a terrible job of hiding the smile. "He's been in the mountains for, like, his whole life and knows his way around. He did horse teams the last couple years."

Oh no, not another one like Old Crusty. "Is he here yet?"

"No. You'll know when Kurt shows up." Rich exchanged a sideways glance with Abigail. "He's kind of hard to overlook."

"Any more generally recognizable features?" I began to imagine Paul Bunyan in ranger green.

"He probably hasn't cut his hair since last fall," Abigail mused. "And you'll hear his bike coming."

Paul Bunyan morphed to "Leather Lloyd." I swallowed. Maybe he had spark plugs instead of deer mice hiding in his beard.

"He's tough as they come. Don't worry, I'm pretty sure he's never actually killed anyone." Rich took a drink out of his pop can, spilling a bit out the side of his mouth.

"I'm sure we would have known. The Chief does screen for

warrants before he hires." Abigail rubbed her upper lip with three finger tips.

"Leather Lloyd" now had Hell's Angels patches all over his black vest. And tattoos. Lots and lots of tattoos.

"He's smart, Abby, I don't think he'd get…. Oh, sorry." Rich grinned at me. "Don't mean to worry you."

Worry, hell. I now had a lump of ice in my gut over the enormous, potentially homicidal biker I was supposed to trust with my life. The whine of a motorcycle cutting through the mumbled conversations meant I had about twenty seconds to run to my car and forget I'd ever wanted to be a ranger.

The bike swung around the corner, drawing to a halt at the side street's curb. I'd been seeing some gigantic Harley chopper with an equally gigantic rider, but the bike was a medium-sized Kawasaki cruiser, and the rider….

He dismounted, leaving his helmet and leather jacket on the bike, and shook out his hair, the only thing that matched my vision of him. Except where I'd been seeing basic brown, he had shoulder-length blond, and where I'd been imagining hardware or rodent-infested snarls on his chin, he was clean-shaven, with strong, sharp features and a dimple at one side of his mouth, he smiled at the group and called greetings.

"Heya, Sid! Mike! Good to see you, Elroy!" He passed through the crowd, exchanging handshakes, backslaps, and the occasional fist bump with a crowd gone suddenly lively. Mrs. Chief hugged him, as did the other female ranger, and he clouted Rich a friendly thump on the arm before pretending to be squished in Abigail's welcome.

"Hi. I'm Kurt Carlson." He stuck a hand out at me, and I shook it, numbed by the vividness that shone from his face. His eyes were the color of the sky, I thought stupidly. Bright blue, must be a reflection, and his smile was like sun breaking through the clouds.

"Jake Landon." I had to think to take back my hand. Oh no. No, no, no. I needed an Old Crusty or a Son of Grizzly Adams, not this man who looked to be a few years older than me, a few inches shorter, a lot more buff, and infinitely more self-possessed.

His grin suddenly dimmed, then came back at half wattage. "Think you're my partner this season."

I'd known him eight seconds and I'd already disappointed him.

"We'll have to talk more, but right now I need to see the Chief." He waved at another late-arriving ranger and disappeared.

"Don't worry, Jake, we were funning you. He is smart and tough, and he's a really nice guy." Abigail patted my arm. "You'll like him."

That's exactly what I was afraid of. I would be drawn to him the same way as this entire crowd was, only more, because I now had a raging lust that demanded to be slaked against his skin, and how was I going to cope with that for an entire summer in a truck with him?

We surged toward the table, where Mrs. Chief was calling us to come and get it. I saw Kurt standing with the Chief by the grill, engaged in what looked like a low, fierce conversation. He looked determined, almost angry, and the Chief wasn't having any. He shook his head and flipped another burger onto the plate. "Make the best of it," I thought I heard the Chief say, and the slump of Kurt's shoulders made me believe it.

Great. He'd known me less than a minute and was already trying to get away. Fine. That would make it really easy to damp down any feelings I might be tempted to have. I'd be his partner in the work, share the chores, and stay in my fucking closet.

The days of orientation crawled by on one level and zipped past on another. Lectures were an extension of the classroom I'd so recently escaped, although any exams would be pass/fail on a practical level, meaning live/dead, injured/whole, or burned/saved. Figuring my best route to impressing my partner was to know my stuff, I mostly kept my attention on the Chief, which worked better when I couldn't actually see Kurt. We used the tanker outside as a laboratory until the Chief was satisfied we could work the radio, gauges, and pumps. The horseback teams practiced with us, since they might need to fight a fire alongside the tanker teams, using our equipment. The presence of the Jeremiah Johnson clones kept me from embarrassing myself.

Abigail found me a couch in her dad's house, so I didn't join the sleepers in the tents that popped up like mushrooms all over the Chief's lawn after the barbecue. I didn't ask where Kurt was sleeping—better I didn't know. I honestly thought he hadn't come back for orientation when I didn't spot a mane of long blond hair the following day, but the muscular stranger with close-cropped hair turned to expose Kurt's killer smile and dimple. The change in style didn't take one iota away from his appeal—it only exposed his high cheekbones.

"I'm going to cut mine too. It's easier to take care of in the mountains," Rich commented when I ran my hand through my own hair, pondering. "Much easier to rinse the shampoo out."

Since my pelt currently resembled a brown bear's, I followed him to the barber shop that evening. Kurt nodded approval next morning and showed me how to adjust the webbing inside my fire helmet.

Too soon for my peace of mind, Kurt had locked his motorcycle into a friend's shed, thrown his sleeping bag into a compartment on our tanker, and given me some quick directions to our cabin. He'd barely spoken with me outside of training, though he'd been friendly enough. Maybe this could work out.

"Can this ride in the car with you?" Kurt had made one last trip into the Chief's house, bringing out some sporting equipment that I barely recognized in its unstrung state.

"Sure." I watched him stow a longbow, a quiver of arrows, and a compound bow crossways inside the car, next to my fishing rod. "Who are you? Robin Hood?"

"Will Scarlet." He turned. "Have you ever shot archery?"

"No." I didn't think plastic bows in middle school gym class counted enough to mention.

"Then you must be Friar Tuck. On to the greenwood." He jumped into the medium-duty truck's cab, the engine rumbled to life, and I followed him out of town.

Friar Tuck indeed. I sucked my gut in for a moment. Goodbye, sedentary student life: hello, adventure.

TWO

Home, sweet home turned out to be a sixteen-by-sixteen-foot square cabin set well back from the stands of trees, close to fifty miles from town. I pulled up next to it where the grass stood thin in last year's tire tracks. The cabin was so tiny that the kitchen and bathroom had to take up most of the floor. The log construction with concrete chinking had to be thick enough to take a foot out of every dimension, and the stone chimney made me wondered how much floor space the hearth took. At least we wouldn't be in there much.

Kurt parked the tanker next to the Toyota and jumped out. "Hey, we got a big place this time!"

"We did?"

"Yes, greenhorn, we did." He shot me a sideways look. "Huge."

"I'm not seeing it." And when I brought in an armload of clothes and sleeping bags, I didn't see anything but a couple of camp cots and a lantern in a single chamber. "Uh...."

Kurt looked at me with some exasperation. "Think. We are

in the middle of a national forest, not suburbia. This is the bedroom, used mostly because we don't like cuddling with elk."

A bedroom that we were sharing. Great. Light began to dawn and got really bright when he led me to the door and around the back. "Part of the bathroom." I looked up at a tank with a pull chain and hoped we had a canvas to stretch between the uprights because privacy and nudity were going to have to go together. "Camp shower. We'll have to rig the hose from the pump at the wellhead to the tank. Shower in the evening if you like it cold, shower in the morning if you like it really cold. Over there"—he pointed to a narrow green hut quite a way from the cabin—"is our privy. Up the hill thataway is part of the kitchen, otherwise known as the 'bear box', and here we have the rest of the kitchen, aka propane stove and picnic table. 'Running water' means you run to get it." He folded one arm across his middle and massaged his temple like I'd given him a headache. "Please tell me the Chief explained this."

"He said 'primitive'. Now I know what primitive looks like." I shrugged. "You said it: we got a huge place." The whole outdoors. I went back to the car for the bags of provisions. Maybe if I kept my head stuck in the trunk for another few minutes, I'd stop glowing. Or I could hide in the bear box with the peanut butter and canned chili. He'd said "No electricity," and I, fool that I was, hadn't considered precisely what that entailed.

I should have put two and two together about the bear box when Kurt and I went shopping. Last night Watt's Ranch Market had been full to overflowing with rangers pushing carts, stocking up on staples and everything else we'd need until our next trip to town:

"Canned roast beef?" I read the label with a certain horror.

"We get back after a long day in the truck, we aren't going

to eat anything that needs hours of cooking." Kurt dumped canned chicken and tuna into the cart next to the bag of cornmeal and the box of powdered eggs, which I'd also questioned. "Powdered stores better than fresh. You just add water."

I shook my head, not questioning the canned peaches, pears, or mixed vegetables, though I did object when Kurt put the sleeve of frozen hamburger patties back. "Those cook fast!"

"They'll be thawed before we ever leave town," he pointed out and tossed them back in the freezer case.

I followed him around, watching some of my selections get shot down, glad other things, including a bag of oranges, got to stay. A trip down the hard goods aisle gave me a close look at the dimple again.

"Yes!" Kurt gloated, playing with the handle on a rotary can opener. "Sharp and new. We need this!" He vanquished an imaginary giant can with a flourish and a snap. "Whatever's in the cabin is probably dull and rusty."

Since our cart contained enough cans to build a pyramid three feet high, I guess we did need it, although buying fresh food would solve the problem too. Kurt put my gallon of milk back in the dairy case anyway.

"Yeah, yeah, the dry milk stores better," I grumbled. He gave me a hairy eyeball when I picked up a block of cheddar cheese, so I put it back and returned the glare when he parked a yellow box of processed plastic cheese next to cans of pinto beans. I was going to have to eat this clown's cooking for the next several months, and he was going to poison me with the raw ingredients before we ever hit the cash register.

The checkout was fraught with its own hazards, such as the little cashier marked "Hi, My Name is Lindy." I was probably the only person in the store who didn't already know. Kurt sure did.

"What are we doing tonight, Kurt?" She looked up at him through her lashes. "I'm nineteen now. You can't say I'm too young this year." She scanned our powdered eggs, making a face at them.

"You're my sweet young thing, Lindy," he assured her. "But not tonight."

"Maybe your hunky partner wants to go bowling." She fluttered her lashes at me from behind wire-framed glasses. "What's your name, hunky partner?"

Hiding behind Kurt wasn't going to help here. "Jake. But I —" I couldn't think of an excuse fast enough.

"He's my ride," Kurt said easily. "Maybe next week?" He took the change she held out, not stroking back when she got more fingertip into the handoff than the coins really needed.

"You're not going out with Tanya, are you? That would really suck if you were going out with Tanya!" Her eyes were imploring.

"No, sweetie, I'm not going out with Tanya." He took an armload of groceries with a wink. "See ya."

Once we deposited everything in the back of the crudmobile, I dared to ask. "Where am I your ride to?"

"Right now, back to the Chief's house." He turned those Colorado blue eyes on me. "She gets off at seven, if you're interested."

"Not. She's kind of aggressive." I had visions of some unwary man laid flat on his back in the parking lot at 7:01 when the little dervish flew out the door.

"She'll be there next week if you change your mind. I thought I'd catch a movie tonight, and not with Tanya. She's got marriage on the brain." He stopped with an air of thoughtfulness. "You could come if you wanted."

I should be somewhere else than sitting in the dark next to him. "Sounds good. Where's the theater?"

"Rifle."

"That's forty miles away. Guess I'd better make a rest stop before we head out." The Chief's house was my best bet. I left the Toyota's motor idling when I went in and stayed in the bathroom long enough to give myself a firm lecture about remaining objective, friendly, and absolutely platonic. I came out to find the motor silent, the hood up, and Kurt bent over the engine.

"What the...?" Bad news. Being too broke to pay repair bills made me afraid to even hear about car problems.

"It stopped. Probably nothing major, but we can't get parts tonight." Kurt dropped the hood with a clang. "We'll take my motorcycle. Deal with it in the morning."

Fretting about the Toyota kept my mind off Kurt. A little. Not much. I had him between my knees, my cock awfully damned close to his ass, for the forty miles of twisty roads down to Rifle. Regretting getting on the bike helped a bit, and not knowing where to put my hands occupied another few brain cells. I had absolutely no memory of the movie afterward, and the ride back had the same issues I'd ridden in with, only more so, because this time I trusted Kurt to keep us upright. The wind in my face was chilly but didn't do a thing to deflate my woody. When he dropped me at Abigail's with the assurances that he could fix the car, I had to peel myself off the back of that motorcycle.

And I swear it was an accident, a bobble while getting my feet off the pegs, but I brushed my groin against Kurt's butt. Brushed my hard and aching cock against him in passing, but it was enough to make a mockery of all my good intentions.

But he didn't show any signs of having noticed, saying only, "See you in the morning" before roaring off into the darkness.

I hoofed it over to the Chief's next morning to find Kurt's butt sticking out of the engine compartment again. Rule One: don't think about patting it. Except to know that, I had to think of patting it. Okay, revised Rule One: Absolutely do not think of Kurt in any sexual way. Off limits. Don't touch. Don't think about touching. Partners only. Friends if we're lucky. "Find the problem?"

"Try it." He tossed the keys at me. The engine turned over at first crank. I would have hugged Kurt out of sheer relief, but —Rule One. No touching. "Great!" I grinned my thanks at him and didn't get out of the car.

"Be right back." He fetched his bows, and we were off. Too bad he'd gotten grease on his utilities, right above the pocket.

We got our homestead put together, folding back the shutters—my job—coaxing the pump into life—Kurt's—filling the shower tank, and lacing the tarp to the uprights to make a stall. I half expected Kurt to laugh at that and suggest skipping it, but he wove the cord through the grommets and tied it tight without comment.

"We need to fill the tank tonight while we've still got daylight, and we'll be ready to go in the morning," Kurt told me. He jumped into the truck with a look of determination that surprised me. The tanker, a medium-duty GMC, had a five-hundred-gallon tank and tool compartments on either side. I hadn't regarded driving it as a problem, but I'd been doing landscaping with the city the last few summers, and the tanker was smaller than the mower haulers.

But hey, he'd done just about everything else under the sun perfectly, so I got in the passenger side, expecting to find out where the water was.

Getting there involved going backward, apparently, and Kurt's knuckles had turned an interesting shade of white before we'd gone twelve feet down the narrow track.

"Swing it right," I advised, but he went the *other* right, way too close to a small pine tree. A hideous scraping sound made him stop, pull forward, and try again. And again.

"Do we still have a Forest Service logo on the side?" I asked through gritted teeth.

"Shut up!" Kurt pulled forward.

"Try putting your hand at the bottom of the steering wheel," I suggested. If he didn't change something, he was only going to bash into that poor tree again.

Which he did. "Damn it all!"

"I thought we were supposed to protect the forest." Okay, I shouldn't have said anything, but watching his mounting frustration, coupled with my relief that he wasn't perfect at everything, came out with laughter.

"If it's so fucking easy, you do it!" Kurt slammed out the driver's door and stood huffing in front of the tanker, hands on his hips.

I slid over, adjusted the mirrors, and avoided that poor abused pine and all its friends on my journey to the little lake that appeared behind the truck. After stopping at water's edge, I cut the motor. I got out to look, studiously ignoring Kurt marching down that track after me. I wouldn't laugh at him, but the corner of my mouth kept twitching.

"Pretty place." I hoped there were fish in here, but it didn't matter. I'd drop a line anyway. It would be a good way to put some space between me and Kurt. The road had been heavily shored up with rocks to prevent erosion and tire tracks where the truck was supposed to back up to the water, but the rest of the lakeside remained untouched. Trees came all the way to the water in a few places. One was tall and sturdy enough to hang a Tarzan rope on. A rim of long grass surrounded most of it, but no real beach touched the water, unless the rocky section leading into the water by the truck ramp counted. The lake was only about sixty yards across, and deep: a beautiful blue jewel set into the mountains.

"Gorgeous." One word for the lake was all Kurt gave me. He dropped the intake hose into the water and stayed on the far side of the truck. Maybe he'd finish seething by the time we sucked up a full tank.

He was sunny again when we pulled the tanker back to the cabin. "'One cooks, one cleans, we take turns' is okay with you?" He produced a coin to flip.

"Fine. I can cook." I felt vaguely obligated to do something to make up for laughing at him, and I also wanted to avoid that processed cheese as long as possible. I'd been feeding myself for years and thought I was pretty good at it, using spices even, but I'd never tried cooking without a proper kitchen.

The can opener had proven its worth and the beans were bubbling on the propane stove when I heard a soft hooting. I'd never seen an owl. I peered into the trees, as confused as the mice about where the predator might be.

"Jake!" Kurt had the pot of beans in both hands, holding it well away from his body lest the boiling sauce splash him. Flames were licking merrily along the propane stove where it had escaped the pot. "Don't turn your back on the stove. You could have started our first fire of the season."

Scorched beans taste like crap. We didn't talk much over dinner, and it was pretty easy to ignore him all night, although his soft noises made me think we had mice or ground squirrels —I tried not to think about skunks—coming into the cabin. We'd be just guys together—I could maintain.

Maintaining got even easier after we got dressed next morning.

"What the hell is that thing on your head?" Kurt eyed my headgear with open skepticism.

I wasn't going to lust after a man who didn't appreciate my bushranger hat.

THREE

I'd been really, really good about keeping my mind off Kurt for the last few weeks, Aussie hat or no Aussie hat, but Rule One was all blown to hell now, watching him standing there in the water falling from the sky. The miniature streams kissed his chest, licked down his arms, and turned me wild with jealousy that I couldn't do the same.

"You want a turn?" he asked, and I shook my head. Hell, yes, I wanted a turn—to pull this heavy coat off, shed the heavy pants, wash off some of the sweat, and press my wet skin to his. I wanted that all the more for having to deny myself even the vaguest daydreams these last few weeks, but I wasn't about to shed the fire suit that was the only armor I had against giving myself away.

"I'll dunk in the lake when we get back," I said and handed the nozzle to him. Trudging back to the truck let me clear a little of the lust and surprise out of my head and think about what had just happened. I cut the pump and started to haul the hose back in.

We would have to work together for another five months.

We'd have to spend time alone in the truck as we patrolled the forest and sleep in the same tiny cabin. A team like ours had to be together a lot, to trust each other a lot, and how the hell was Kurt going to trust me if he knew how much I wanted him? I thought I'd had it all under control, and I was wrong.

I threw my protective jacket and pants into the cargo bin and retrieved my bush hat before starting more labor in the sun. Kurt hadn't stopped giving me crap about the hat, so I pulled it low over my brow.

The effort of coiling the hose might push down the hunger I felt, or at least let my throbbing erection calm down. Doing something about it wasn't going to happen, and I had to get back under control.

Squishing the water out of the hose made the rigid thing go soft and limp, which was more than was happening for me. I couldn't stop thinking of how Kurt looked in the sun: wet, glistening, happy, and totally at ease to be standing half naked on a Colorado mountaintop.

Since we came up to the cabin, we'd become friends. Nice platonic friends who didn't spend every waking moment wanting to grab one another's asses. Which worked better if I didn't look at him closely, because I was afraid that just this thing would happen. Watching him stand in the water falling out of the sky made him impossible to ignore, and the rivulets running over his face and down his chest only outlined the handsome features and hard body until I couldn't *not* look at him anymore.

Think about heaving the hose. Think about anything besides your partner with no T-shirt on, laughing in the spray. I yanked savagely on the hose as I coiled it and tried to ignore Kurt moving around the truck, stowing equipment and radioing in the details to headquarters. It would be at least a half-hour ride back to the cabin and the tiny lake next to it. I'd have to jump in the lake when we got there—it would be more effective than a cold shower, which I needed, badly.

At least I could shift my erection to the least conspicuous position before going around to the side of the truck. The loose utility pants were my only friend today, and even they wouldn't be enough help. My hard-on was never inconspicuous, I was too big for that, but I couldn't let Kurt know I was stiff. I thought about fires and dentists and how much it hurt when the damned camp cot pinched my hand this morning, but it wasn't until I got to the thought of eating canned roast beef that I finally calmed down enough to risk getting in the truck with Kurt.

He nearly undid it all, though, as he mopped his face with his shirt before shrugging back into it. Usually, the dusty forest-green T-shirt that was our working uniform at least covered up his chest. I caught the sight out of the corner of my eye as I tried to look at something on the other side of the valley instead.

"You okay, Jake?" he asked, and I grunted something back about "yeah, sure, fine." Telling the truth here was out of the question.

I tried to keep up my end of the conversation on the way back to the cabin, because tired or not, Kurt wanted to talk. Jazzed from the fire, Kurt went on and on about our little smolder, and how he'd put out similar fires in the last two years. Then he wanted to quiz me. "Did we follow the Ten Standard Fire Orders?"

"I think so, as much as we could maintain organizational control with only the two of us. It's not like we could post lookouts, exactly." I'd learned the standard orders in orientation; they'd been on handouts, which I could look at on my own time. "We had escape routes, we knew the weather conditions, knew what the fire was doing and what it could be expected to do under current conditions, we thought clearly, acted decisively, and fought aggressively."

"You missed a couple," he prompted.

"Some of your instructions weren't too clear."

"What was unclear about 'Push'?" he wanted to know.

I thumped his arm—maybe he'd stop.

"Okay, did we have any Watch Out situations? You've got eighteen choices."

"No, unless you felt like taking a nap near the fire line and didn't mention it. Aren't you taking this mentor role a little too seriously?" I really was ready for him to stop: I couldn't think clearly enough to play Twenty Questions about fires just now. My sore back twinged. I gave it a sympathetic rub, promising myself that cold water would help ease the ache.

"It's your life and mine, Jake." He launched into a discussion of why we'd done what we'd done, and I listened to him, trying to pay particular attention to the technical bits about crown fires and burnovers. I missed half of this back when the Chief mentioned it during orientation.

I'd been distracted then, and for the same reasons it was hard to concentrate now. A dozen rangers jammed into the living room didn't leave a lot of space for the Chief to pace around up by the blackboard. After stepping on someone's feet, he finally growled at us to scoot back. The few who'd scored furniture to sit on had more company than they might have liked, although Rich didn't look too unhappy about Abigail sitting on his lap. I ended up on the arm of the couch, trying not to kick anyone in the head. Swinging my legs stopped abruptly in the great shuffle: Kurt and another man had my legs pinned against the couch.

I wanted to be attentive—this was only the technicalities of my new job—but with Kurt's close-cropped blond head by my knees, I think I heard one word out of three. The rest got lost in the warmth of his back, even through a layer of jersey and another of denim.

So now I could fill in the gaps with a personal tutor, and I could even pay a smidge more attention since he wasn't touching me. Except for the friendly punches against my arm when I was too slow to answer his questions, or couldn't.

"No, dodo," Kurt said, thunking me again. "You heard the Chief. Take down the ladder fuel so the fire doesn't climb into the crowns. Jeez, you're going to kill someone with pills if you pay attention like that in pharmacy school." He'd nodded and said, "Huh," when I'd confided my plans, and I didn't think he'd been listening. Should have known better.

"I'm not going to be dog-tired like this in pharmacy school." I thunked him back, knowing he was right, but I didn't think I'd be facing the same distractions there either. Oh crap, that was another hit on Rule One. "I knew the Ten Standard Fire Orders, didn't I?"

Kurt turned us down the dirt fire road that led to our cabin. "You know, Jake, they teach us all about this stuff so when the worst happens, we're prepared. But they can't possibly teach us what we really need for this job."

"What's that?"

"It's how to be at ease in our own heads so we can do the patrolling without going nuts."

Please don't mention nuts, I thought. Mine were going to be aching. "Yeah," I managed to answer. "We might go days quietly patrolling, which would be good, but it's a lot of peace and quiet between the active parts." It was very peaceful in the mountains. The only people we'd seen all day were each other and a guy on a Harley Fat Boy with a sleeping bag and some other gear on the back, zipping down one of the roads and scaring the wildlife with the noise. Not that we could hear the meadowlarks sing or the grasshoppers buzz over the rumble of the diesel, but was a guy on a bike that loud really getting more of a nature experience than catching bugs with his teeth?

Kurt pulled up next to the cabin and turned to me. "You don't seem too at ease right now. The fire bothering you?"

He'd noticed. It was too much to hope that a guy who made his living by noticing things would not notice that I wasn't my usual self.

Except I was. I was stuffing down everything like I always did. I'd stuffed down my desire for men all my life, and I would stuff down the desire I felt for Kurt. We had to get along for months yet, and I refused to screw that up by telling him he aroused me like no one else in the world. Ignoring my feelings was just harder to do with him turned in the seat of the truck to look at me with serious blue eyes.

"No, it isn't." That much was the truth. Then I had an inspiration. "I'm trying to figure out what I can make for dinner without poisoning you."

"Oh, no. It is your night to cook," he groaned.

One of these days I'd live down those burnt beans. "I could fry up some Spam in a brown sugar sauce with some of those canned peas."

"Oh, no. No, no, no." He looked faintly queasy. "If those peas were that good, the guys would have eaten them last year and not left them for us."

"Okay, the peas suck, but there isn't anything else green in the bear box. Wish there was a salad in there. Or a watermelon." My teeth suddenly ached for something cold and crisp.

"But you made Spam last week and it was okay." As okay as Spam could ever be.

"We had butter last week, and I didn't give you peas." Kurt looked thoughtful now, and then he smiled broadly. His dimple showed, that damned dimple that I'd about convinced myself to ignore. "I have a better idea. I'll take your turn to cook, and you take the truck down to the lake and refill the tank."

I could get my chilly dip, top off the tank, and maybe clear my head at the same time. At the very least I'd be more than two feet away from Kurt, not close enough to reach over and touch that dimple. I wanted to touch that dimple in the worst way. "It's a deal."

FOUR

When Kurt jumped out of the tanker, I watched him amble into the cabin before I slid over and threw the truck back into gear. The seat still bore the impression of his body. I wasn't too sure who'd gotten the better end of the deal, although the truck should have been pleased.

The engine sounds probably scared off all the animals, but I checked for movement across the water anyway. A small stream fed the lake with snowmelt—deer liked to come down to the water there. I'd watched them pick their way to the shore on my nights there with the fishing rod and stayed to see the stars come out. The sky doesn't look like that in the city, where there are too many competing lights. In the wilderness, it's like it must have been thousands of years ago, when men started naming the constellations. I loved the lake; it was one of the great joys of being out here.

Now I could drop the intake hose into the water, start the pump, and take my clothes off. No line of sight between the narrow shore and the cabin would give me away—the trees were too thick—so I had some privacy to get wet. I needed it because I'd made the mistake of remembering the way Kurt looked with streams of water running over his bare chest and shoulders, glistening droplets in his hair, and the way he smiled with his lips parted and his eyes closed as the cool water fell on his upturned face. I wondered if he looked like that in bed, then I was erect again.

I was hard and naked and I had two choices. I could throw myself into a snow-fed lake and cool my lust by force, or I could take matters in hand and enjoy myself first, and then throw myself in the lake to get clean. Guess which one I chose.

Imagining running my tongue over his collarbone and licking up the water there got me started, and then I could kiss my way over his neck to suck up more. The thought of putting my mouth to his skin made me put my hand on my cock, and I anticipated more intimate caresses while I stroked. His brown nipples would need kissing and licking, too, making me wonder how hard I'd need to suck to pull one into my mouth. Inexperience stank, but imagination made up for it, and at least I knew what I was doing with myself. I wouldn't last long, not the way I imagined pulling Kurt close and pressing my own bare chest against his wet body. When I thought of him putting that smiling mouth onto my skin, I came, and it nearly buckled my knees.

When I could move again, I checked the gauge on the truck. It needed to point to five hundred gallons, and it wasn't there yet. In a few more minutes I'd have to cut the pump, but I had time to jump into the cold water. I needed to get my shit together if I was going to go back to the cabin and not act guilty. Scrubbing myself with my hands, I tried to get as much smoke and sweat off as I could without soap.

The camp shower we had set up by the cabin worked okay; the cistern that we filled from the well let the water warm in the sun. Kurt might be taking a relatively warm—as in twenty-five degrees warmer than the lake, but thirty degrees colder than a water heater—shower even now. A truly hot shower was a luxury for when we stopped by headquarters, or on the occasions we swung by Rendezvous Lake Lodge, where we were welcomed as friends.

Warm water was for wusses and guys who weren't trying to banish a raging case of lust. I ducked completely below the surface again and came up shivering. The cold water made me gasp and tingle—it felt like my balls were trying to crawl back up into my body before they froze off.

The sound of the pump changed from a steady chugging to a distressed clank. The cold water had done its work on me, and the malfunction gave me a reason to get out of the water before my balls climbed all the way to my pancreas to get warm. With a snort, I pulled the hose up out of the water—more carefully once I found the source of the problem. A cutthroat trout had gotten near enough to get pulled against the opening and now thrashed in a fruitless effort to free itself. It had grown to a size uncommon in more heavily fished waters, big enough to block the intake hose.

When I cut the pump, it fell to the ground, but I was fast enough to catch it and dispatch it. Extracting a big brush knife from one of the truck's tool compartments gave me something to use for a boning knife, and I smiled in satisfaction. Coated with oil and rolled in cornmeal, that trout would sizzle up in the pan and be a fine, fine addition to whatever Kurt threw together. We worked hard today, and we'd be hungry enough to finish the fish and everything else, too. Best of all, Kurt would have to eat his words about my cooking.

I came up the hill ready to park near the cabin, when my attention zeroed in on Kurt, who was waving his arms, throwing rocks, and screaming loud enough to be heard, barely, over the rumble of the truck. He'd gone halfway up the track to the bear box. The object of his wrath stood at the metal chest where we stored the food, ignoring the rocks that didn't come within yards of hitting.

A brown bear held something in his paws, munching away, not very concerned by the commotion. A lot of debris lay around his feet; he'd had enough time to clear out most of our stores, including the box of powdered eggs, judging from the yellow streaks over his face.

Bet he liked those better than I did, but that didn't mean he could march up and scarf the lot. I threw the truck in gear and headed for the bear box, though the track was pretty narrow. I came bounding up the track, hitting the horn and hoping to scare the daylights out of the bear—but alarming Kurt just as much. He leaped to one side and then chased the truck to where I finally ran out of track by the box.

Frightened at last, the intruder retreated, but not fast enough to suit Kurt, who yanked the hose off the rack and hit the pump. Still screaming, he aimed the nozzle at the ursine bandit, knocking it to the ground with the force of the water. It picked itself up and ran much faster after that. I blasted the horn at its retreating butt, as much from anger as for frightening the bear, though it should have been terrified at the things Kurt was yelling.

"Damn you all to hell gonna use your hide for a rug and pick my teeth with your bones furry rat bastard goddamn bear!" He finally wound down as the bear became a speck in the distance. "Don't come back!" Glowering, he coiled the hose once more.

I started picking up what remained of our stores. It wasn't much: some peas, peaches, Spam, and half a jar of jam. Our last loaf of bread had been partially chewed, and the box of crackers had a couple of punctures. None of the other odds and ends were unscathed. Most of the cornmeal dusted the ground. I latched the box and rattled the handle, casting nervous glances into the distance in case the bear remembered he was a lot bigger than us. Kurt did the same, grumbling that he'd done it right earlier.

I had to back the truck to the cabin once again, because there was no good way to turn around. Kurt sat beside me, fuming, during the long trek backward.

"It's going to be a pretty lean dinner, Jake. Spam and canned peas are what we have left," Kurt said, and it was worth eating the peas to see his face when I produced the enormous trout.

An hour or so later, Kurt and I sat down to plates of fried fish and green blobs.

"That was fun," Kurt observed gloomily, pushing the peas around on his plate. "Not."

"Hey, we salvaged some stuff." The trout was really, really good. I took another crispy, flaky bite and chewed blissfully.

"Joy. Half a loaf of bread, a box of crackers, half a dozen cans of things we don't really want to eat. The bastard got the new jar of peanut butter." He catapulted a pea off his fork into a clump of mountain mahogany. "I could swear I latched the bear box properly this morning."

"That was not your average bear, Boo Boo."

"At least the box is far enough from the cabin for good camp hygiene. The bears don't come down to peek in the windows if we don't keep food here to attract them." He took a bite of trout, which I had cooked in the last of the unlicked cornmeal, and his face softened.

"Then quit trying to attract them with peas. You mentioned

not liking to sleep with the elk, but…." I didn't like this next thought. "Is the cabin strong enough to keep a bear out?"

"Not if he really wants in," Kurt admitted, shifting a little on the bench. "And does anything in the world eat canned peas except in an emergency?"

I decided it wasn't an emergency and shoved my peas to one side. "You were standing there throwing rocks and screaming at it. Kurt, what if it ran to you instead of away from you?" I was suddenly glad that we bear-boxed the trash and packed it out. Leftover peas and all.

He looked abashed but not chastened. "I wouldn't have done it if we were up by Yellowstone. Those bears aren't wary of people. But real wilderness bears—"

"Have long fangs and longer claws," I interrupted. "And I know I don't have to outrun the bear, I only have to outrun you, but since I'm not sure I could, would you mind not doing such a dumb-ass thing again?" The adrenaline had already taken me from high to hangover; tonight I'd sleep very soundly, if I didn't dream of furry faces at the window.

"But it wasn't a park bear."

"Imagine all the paperwork you'd have to do if you misplaced me like that."

"Oh, Lord. In triplicate." He moaned and changed the subject on me. "We're going to have to figure out what to do until we get into town."

"Can't we just go tomorrow?" Socks didn't have to wait for Tuesdays to get clean, and the market would take our money any day.

"Nope—Tomorrow's Rich and Abigail's day. We cover for them, they cover for us. Can't let two sections go bare. We're stuck with waiting 'til the day after tomorrow," Kurt explained around a mouthful of fish.

The trout was disappearing into us at a remarkable rate. "Canned peas for breakfast?"

Kurt mashed some peas flat with his fork. "Great. We'll figure something out."

"We will. There's a couple of cans of other things." I had a wonderful thought. "Oh, and Kurt, I don't want to hear another word about burnt beans."

FIVE

The next day we were both pretty quiet. I didn't think Kurt had seen me taking matters in hand at the lake—thanks to the bear and the thick trees I shouldn't really worry—but my guilty conscience whispered to me. He was a really nice guy, one of the easiest people to be with I'd ever met, and if I wasn't careful, I would mess with that. He might have been fretting about the bear box.

Usually, we could talk about anything and everything. We both travelled a bit, which gave us common ground, and we'd had some similar experiences in college, though he razzed me about the granola life at the University of Colorado. He was three years older than my twenty-two, and he'd used the time to have adventures I never imagined and to collect better stories. I didn't have anything that compared to spending two days in a bivvy bag, clinging to the side of El Capitan because a storm raging through Yosemite had caught him and his climbing partner halfway up the mountain.

"I thought he was going to kill me." Kurt had joked about it last week. "We were roped in pretty close, had to be, because it kept less of us exposed to the rain and the ledge was narrow. I'd eaten some really pungent salami. He bitched about my meat breath, which I couldn't fix any more than I could fix the rain. Kind of killed the friendship. We didn't go climbing together again."

He'd gone pensive after that, and I thought about that as we patrolled the forest, up and down the dirt roads. I didn't want to risk what was between us—I wanted to take things to a new level. But I didn't know how to do that, and I was scared to death that what I really wanted to do would be the end of *our* friendship. Not every man wants to be touched by another man, and I didn't know what Kurt wanted. I felt like an idiot. I couldn't even ask, because asking might cause exactly what I wanted to avoid. He might demand to be reassigned.

We patrolled in silence, and I tried to pretend that driving the truck absorbed my attention completely.

So the Boy Scout troop kind of took me by surprise.

Six or seven of them, ages roughly ten to twelve, and a couple of adult leaders were standing by the side of the road, waving at us. Instead of waving back, we stopped, because we needed to know who ran loose in our woods making campfires. Good public relations, too, but knowing where the trouble could start was a lot more important.

This sort of stop was kind of fun; we'd talk to all the campers and hikers we met. We would chat with the group, ask them what they were doing and where they were headed, how long they'd be out. One of the leaders nodded approvingly at me for checking with the boys instead of the adults.

"Want to see the rig?" Kurt asked. A pack of uniform-clad boys instantly swarmed the truck.

"You really wear these?" The shortest Scout put Kurt's jacket and helmet on. His hands didn't show at the ends of the sleeves. "How can you work in this?"

Another Scout took the helmet and an axe, which he didn't swing at an imaginary tree until he was well away from the group. Still, the leader put a stop to that, making the other boys heft the blade without chopping.

"The weight of the axe helps take the trees down, but it's a good workout," I said as I retrieved the axe and handed out shovels. My lower back still ached from the previous day's exertions. The boys dug and tossed the dirt at a gambel oak Kurt designated as a fire until everyone had taken a turn and the "fire" was "out."

The boys wanted to see what we stocked in the first aid kit, and one asked, "What good does a stretcher do if there's only two of you?"

"Good question. We call other rangers for backup if it's a big blaze." I stepped back out of the way of the two boys who loaded a third on the stretcher and marched off with him. The rest clamored for rides, too, investigating one of our fire shelters while they waited. We'd opened one to let them crawl in and imagine what it would be like to huddle in what looked like an oversized, foil-covered sleeping bag while flames raged outside of the flimsy structure.

"It keeps enough heat out and enough oxygen in that you have a pretty good chance of surviving a burnover," Kurt explained. "You want to be down low, where the temperatures are lowest and there's the least smoke. How long the fire takes to burn out around you depends on what kind of fuel it has. If there's a lot of woody stuff, you could be in there a while."

"Can't you just stay in the truck?" one of the Scouts suggested after he popped the hatch and rolled out of the confined space. He gave the shelter a horrified look and then hastened to fasten the hatch when one of the others got in, prompting a squawk and a "Hey!" from me.

Kurt flinched. "No. Bad idea. The windshield can break and let all the flames in there with you, and the fumes that come out of a burning dashboard will chase you right out into the fire. If the fuel system catches fire, you're sitting on a large bomb." The boys looked at him with horror, and I could understand—the truck had looked like a refuge to me until the Chief explained. "We use the shelters."

"Ever put it to the test?" asked one of the Scout leaders as he squatted down to look inside.

"No, not yet," Kurt replied. A barely perceptible shudder passed over him.

The leader pinched the wall of the shelter, which really was sturdier than the tin foil it resembled. I hoped. Suddenly I wasn't so sure. "That's too much like a human campfire dinner for me," he said.

I could have done without that image; I might need to use that shelter one day. We did get the dang thing refolded with only one muttered curse about government-issue equipment.

We showed them the water tank and explained how we filled it and when we'd use it. "Five hundred gallons won't stop much of a fire, but it can be useful, and it will buy us a little time to call in the other guys. If there's a water source near enough, we'll put the intake down and pump straight from the stream or lake and bypass the tank, conserving it for when we need it. We spend a lot of time driving around, looking for the fires while they're still smoldering quietly and making more smoke than trouble. We put one of those out yesterday," Kurt told them, and they looked impressed.

One of the boys worried aloud. "That wasn't started by a campfire, was it?"

"No, no sign of a campfire. Most of these fires are started by lightning, not campers, though Smoky Bear has a point about prevention," I explained, and then fixed them with a steely glare. "You guys have been using good campfire techniques, haven't you?"

They fell over themselves to assure us that they had been very careful, but I wasn't taking anyone's word for it. "Over there, dudes. Work in teams of three. Show me how you do it."

So the boys built fire rings with rocks and cleared the ground around them of pine needles and anything else that would burn. They built tinder and kindling teepees, though I didn't let them light up, and when they'd satisfied me, they covered the "coals" with dirt to douse them.

"All right, then," Kurt said. "You guys want to try squirting the hose?" Loud cries of "Yeah!" greeted this suggestion. We pulled it out and showed them what to do.

"Point it here," Kurt told the first in line, "and you hold on, too," he told the second boy. "Hang on tight." They still wouldn't be adequately prepared for the jolt when I hit the pump. The kid blasted a hole in the ground at first, but then aimed it up, and when he switched off, the next one pointed the hose upward. The water came down with only gravity's speed, reminding me of how Kurt and I had done this yesterday, and I think he was thinking of it, too, because he flashed a smile at me that damn near melted my boots.

The Scouts took their turns, then the leaders took the hose and let the boys dance in the falling water, whooping as they got soaked. We had to call a halt to the fun before they were ready but before the tank went dry, and packed up and sent them on their way.

"I topped off last night, you know," I said, reading the gauges. The bear and the boys had gotten close to half a tank.

"It's a good excuse to head out toward Rendezvous Lake," he replied. "We can refill there and get lunch at the lodge."

"Oh, yeah. Maybe Max has some ribs ready!" The proprietor of the Rendezvous Lake Lodge made some of the most mouthwatering ribs I'd ever tasted. Last week Kurt had ordered the last serving before informing me how good they really were. He'd eaten partway through the rack, making "mmm…" noises, before relenting and handing one over. The threat of burning his beans deliberately had parted him from just the one, and it was so good that I was sure only threats would have made him share.

"It will be worth shaking our kidneys loose on that dirt road if he does." Kurt grinned. "Wonder if we can convince the county to grade it again." Somehow the truck had pointed itself toward the Rendezvous Lake Lodge as we talked. "You were pretty good with the Scouts back there, turning into old Smoky Bear with your hands on your hips, grilling them about fire pits."

"I don't want them making any stupid mistakes." I steered around a rather large rock that protruded from the middle of the roadbed, where the softer soil was wearing away around it.

"No. Though maybe you looked more like a drill sergeant, with the tight green T-shirt tucked into the fatigue pants, and that hat."

"Lay off the hat. I like this hat." I tipped it down over one eye, aiming for the rakish effect.

"You need a marsupial on your shoulder with that hat—isn't that why the brim turns up on one side?" He batted up at the brim, tipping it back on my head. "Colorado is fresh out of koala bears, but we could get the Scouts to find you a possum."

"I don't need a possum!" I readjusted the brim to level.

"Sure you do, if you're going to wear an Aussie bush hat." Kurt was having way too much fun with this.

"It'll play dead and fall off anyhow." I hoped it would; I didn't want its fifty teeth near my ear or its naked, prehensile tail wrapped around my neck. Too much like having a twelve-pound rat on your shoulder.

"And you need to say 'crikey' a lot." The dimple mocked me as he laughed at his own joke. "Come on, say it. 'Crikey'!"

"No, and I'm not going to say 'Isn't she a beauty?' either." I gave him a sour, sideways glance, wondering why his smile softened.

He begged, "Just one 'Crikey'?"

"No!" The joke was wearing thin for me. "What I will do is sing 'Waltzing Matilda' for you. I know the whole thing. 'Once a jolly swagman…'."

I had him pleading for mercy before I got to the line with the boiling billy. That'd teach him.

Friendship and superior barbecue were enough to pull us down the road toward the Rendezvous Lake Lodge, run by Kurt's buddy Max, who knew what was going on over most of the area and didn't mind sharing. We passed Deerhaven Lodge at what would have been lunchtime, but weren't tempted to turn in. One of these days, we'd have to find out what their specials were. On a day Max had no ribs.

At around one thirty, we pulled into the Rendezvous's main parking lot, which was empty except for a red RAV4 loaded with camping gear. A man wrestled with a cooler that resisted loading into the back seat, getting no help from a sulky girl in shorts and a hoodie who leaned against a front fender, taking deep drags on her cigarette. Tobacco smoke warred with the tantalizing odor of grilled pork and burgers wafting from the kitchen. We wrinkled our noses against the foul cigarette odor, which didn't dissipate fast enough when she threw the butt on the ground and stamped it out with her foot. There were another half dozen butts scattered on the dirt parking lot near her.

"Hello, fellas." Max came out onto the veranda to greet us. "Miss, pick those up." His tone was firm but polite, yet it didn't stir the girl into action. "Miss, now, please."

"Yeah, yeah, sure." She left one behind when she threw the butts into the sand-filled ashtray to the right of the lodge door.

"All of them," Max prodded, arms crossed. With his salt and pepper hair, horn rim glasses, and air of authority, he looked like somebody's father who damned well expected to be obeyed. She did get the last butt, throwing it into the receptacle with an exaggerated motion.

"Happy now?" She lit another cigarette, eyes slitted against the smoke.

"I'd be happier if I didn't worry about you doing that where the stuff on the ground burns," Max told her.

"Smoky Bear, only you, yadda yadda yadda. *I'd* be happier if I wasn't going off to spend three days in the woods bonding with Pops, who thinks that I need electricity deprivation therapy." She jerked her thumb savagely at the man, who backed out of the vehicle. He had the air of one who was reconsidering plans—perhaps electricity therapy applied with a Taser would do more to adjust her attitude.

"Where in the woods?" Kurt asked her with a smile that suggested he'd brave deep dark forests to join her, but she was having none of it.

"Who the hell knows? It's all trees to me." She jumped into the passenger seat and slammed the door hard enough to make the little SUV shake.

"Sorry about that. All the fresh air seems to be affecting her brain. We don't really have a set destination." Her father got into the driver's seat and cranked the engine, leaving us shaking our heads.

"They had a cabin for the week, but she kept stinking it up with her cigarettes, so I asked them to leave," Max told us during the brief walk to the nearly empty dining room. "They didn't rent a canoe, they didn't want horses, and she kept demanding television, so they weren't providing anywhere near enough revenue to put up with the reek. I told them when they booked that the electricity goes off at nine."

"I thought the customer was always right," I said, knowing that he'd explode.

"Not hardly, and they're welcome to try getting a room elsewhere. It's only seventeen miles down my rotten dirt road and then eight miles over to Deerhaven, and I can tell you they're booked solid, so it will be woods or head home for them. Folks can behave or get out, and I don't mind telling them that." Max snorted. "So, do I even need to ask what you want this time, or should I just dish up the ribs?" He'd laughed at us last week as teasing turned to begging and begging turned to threats.

"Start dishing!" Kurt answered for both of us, and pretty soon plates of fragrant meat showed up in front of us. There's no way to eat ribs without diving in up to your elbows, and we'd need every one of the huge stack of napkins Max brought us.

Oh, that meat was heavenly. Tangy with molasses, tomato, and smoke, nearly falling off the bone, and better than anything we'd eaten since the platter last week—including last night's trout, good as it had been. We dove in, too hungry to talk, and it wasn't until I devoured close to half the rack that I even looked up. I should have looked back down, but Kurt was enjoying his food so much that I had to shake myself not to stare. He sliced off a rib and put it to his mouth, then closed his eyes and chewed. Then he had to get the shreds of meat off the bone, along with the last drops of sauce, using lips, teeth, and tongue. He flat out enjoyed that rib more than I have ever seen anyone enjoy food.

As he cleaned that bone, I had a sudden flash of what it might be like to have his mouth on something else long and hard, in some place a lot more private than a dining room. I gulped and tried to turn back to my coleslaw and potato salad, but the image stayed with me.

All of a sudden, I wasn't hungry any more. I excused myself and headed to the men's room. I had to remember to wash my hands when I went in, because otherwise I was going to have barbecue sauce all over my fly.

SIX

The smell of mesquite-smoked barbecue traveled around with us the rest of the day, which didn't have anything more in the way of adventures. I had to pack the rest of my lunch up to take along, and Max had fixed us a care package for dinner. We stopped to chat with some hikers, and that was about it for civilization. The view was pine trees, spruce trees, more pine trees, a clump of aspens here and there, and the occasional meadow. We couldn't really see the mountains for being in them, but the twist of the roads did let us see higher peaks now and then. Still a lot of snow up top, though it was melting with the summer.

"Fire danger is pretty low now," Kurt mused, "but everything dries out in the summer and it will increase." We passed a fire danger sign beside the road as we drove away from Rendezvous Lake. The semicircular dial's hand pointed to the blue of "low," but as the season advanced, we'd be the ones to change the reading. It could very well get to the yellow section of "very high" or even the red of "extreme," when a hot look could start a blaze, before the snows came again. "We're the lucky guys who get to inform the campers that they can't build a fire when that happens. Half of them don't bring propane stoves, and they get really cranky."

"I bet. Does Max stock propane stoves at the lodge gift shop?"

"Bet he does." Kurt laughed. "We could point people his way. Then their trips wouldn't get ruined."

I looked out the window at the woods, green shading to black in the shadows. "At least we don't have a lot of beetle-killed pines, like down toward Winter Park." Entire hillsides showed dead brown and blue-gray along the highway between Empire and Granby, hundreds of acres. Some were clear cut of dead trees, leaving stubble and branches, land that wouldn't recover for decades. I'd been horrified when I drove up from Boulder for orientation, thinking that I'd be patrolling more of the same, but the forest here had undergone no such devastation.

Kurt shook his head. "Now, there's a disaster waiting to happen. That stuff will go up like a torch."

"Why is it a problem down there and not up here?" I could see two dead trees in a sea of green.

"Winters are still so cold up here that it keeps the beetles in check," Kurt said as he turned down the road to our cabin. "We'll lose a tree here and there, that's all."

Our one-room cabin sat in an artificial clearing, the trees cut back to a safe distance because of the fire danger. My battered old Toyota sat to one side, and the picnic table lay in the shadow of the building now, though it caught the morning sun. Kurt pulled the truck into its spot around the back of the cabin, and I grabbed the food. We'd eat outdoors.

"I'll get some forks!" Kurt grinned as he went to the door.

I placed the take-out dishes on the table, glad to be home. This place felt like home because I was going to eat dinner with him. Kurt: my friend, my companion, but not my lover. I didn't know how to reach out to him without destroying the friendship.

The leftovers tasted wonderful, even cold, and we were licking up the last drops of sauce when Kurt spoke again. "There's a bit of light left, so I think I'll head over to the archery range, shoot a couple of quivers with the compound bow. Want to join me?"

Hell, yes. "Might. Or I might go for a quick swim." A good dunking would substitute for the cold shower I was afraid I'd need again.

"Suit yourself," he said, crumpling up his tin foil plate and paper napkins, which we'd have to pack out with the rest of the trash when we went to town. "You need the practice."

I did. Kurt was a good shot with both the compound bow that he used for hunting and the recurve bow that Robin Hood would have given his hood for. Kurt himself would be a fine addition to the Merry Men. He'd look good in the green tights, with a feathered cap set jauntily over one blue eye. I'd joined him at the range a time or two, but since cultivating my artificial disinterest in Kurt practically required me to spend my evenings by the lake, I hadn't achieved any particular skill.

"I'll bring the recurve bow if I come down." I didn't want to promise anything, and a bit of space would be a good thing, especially tonight. "But I think I'll swim."

The "archery range" consisted of a couple of hay bales and a target set up against a hillside about a hundred yards away from the cabin. The hill caught the stray arrows (mine), and the aspens provided a dappled background for Kurt to hone his eye for bow-hunting season.

I watched him leave with the compound bow and couldn't decide what to do.

Sitting at the picnic table with my face in my hands, I debated following him down to the archery range. Was it my imagination, or had he looked hurt when I didn't opt to join him right off? We'd been together all day—surely he didn't want even more of my company. The cold swim seemed like a better idea than usual tonight. It took a long time to make up my mind.

But when I went in to get a towel to take to the lake, I picked up the recurve bow instead.

I followed the path we'd made down to the meadow and thought about how good Kurt looked as he left: muscular shoulders with a bow slung over and tight buttocks flexing inside his dusty, green utility pants. That nearly made me turn around and head back to the lake because I suddenly wanted to put my hands on those buttocks and squeeze.

If I hadn't been so nearly there, I might have turned around, but instead, I looked over across the meadow to the target. I had yet to emerge from the trees, so Kurt couldn't see me even if he was looking, but he wasn't; he was intent on what he was doing.

I never expected to see him do *this*.

SEVEN

Kurt must have decided I wasn't coming after all, because he had pulled his T-shirt over his head so that it stretched across his back. He was facing to the right, leaning against an aspen tree, and now he slid his utilities down over his thighs.

I held my breath and froze as he revealed his body, his cock already standing tall. He had to think he was completely alone, since I'd taken so long. He'd had time to shoot the full quiver. A dozen arrows were sticking out of the hay bale target, and he must have gotten sidetracked when he went to retrieve them. His bare chest was pale under the tanned hand stroking his skin. With his other hand he stroked back up his thigh toward his hard cock. The utility pants stayed around his knees as he touched himself in the dappled light. Patches of shadows from the moving aspen leaves danced over his skin like caresses—I absolutely had to look.

The sleeves, which were the only part of that shirt he was exactly wearing, stretched over sculpted biceps that rippled with his movements. Shadows flickered between the whipcords in his forearms and picked out the muscles in his otherwise flat belly.

His was the body of a man who labored, having definition and purpose. Totally beautiful, totally male, totally desirable. His erection curved up, pointing toward his belly, bringing my own cock to stiffness as I looked.

I wanted to go. I wanted to go away and leave him to his solitary pleasure. And oh, how I wanted to go to him and touch him. Frozen in place, I could only watch Kurt grip his hard cock at the base and pinch one nipple. How much pressure did he like? I couldn't tell from here, and I suddenly needed to know, because I wanted to do it for him.

I remained hidden in the trees while my own cock throbbed with need. I would stay over here, and I'd watch and mirror what he was doing, because I wanted to touch him so badly. Mirroring what he did to himself might be as close as I could ever get.

My own T-shirt went over my head and across my back, my pants went down around my knees. Eight inches of hard cock in my own hand, and I had to lean against a tree to stay upright. Wanting to believe that my hand was his wrapped around my erection, I matched his slow strokes. Imaging my erection was his, I thought about touching him, holding his length in my hand. My eyes were open just enough to see what Kurt did across the clearing, and I did the same, trying to be both of us, trying to feel both of us as I touched myself the way he touched himself.

When he left off pinching his nipple, so did I, and trailed my hand over my chest and stomach the way he did. When he picked up speed, pumping his full, thick cock, so did I, and wanted to memorize the pace because if this is what he liked, I wanted to give it to him. If it would only be in my memory, with my own hand on my own cock later, I wanted it to be the way he liked it. From our opposite sides of the clearing, I stroked him and tried to feel his hands on me.

What was he doing now? His shoulder pressed against the tree, and he'd tossed his head back beside the trunk—he looked the way he had the other day in the water. My own hand went faster, and I had to slow myself—I didn't want to come before him. A firm grip at my base chased the orgasm back. He'd caressed his chest and belly as he stroked his rigid length—now he drew that hand across his torso and down his flank. It went behind him, and I remembered how I'd wanted to grab his ass, so I grabbed my own and wished I could see what he was really doing. The muscles moved under my skin as I wondered.

I knew what I was doing; I was thinking of how one buttock in each hand would feel. I wanted to hold his cheeks, spread them gently, and probe the little hole that nestled between them. I would put a finger there. Maybe two. I'd touch my hard cock there and press in, or would he rather be the one to do it to me? I'd never done either one, but I wanted to like never before—I had to strangle the moans that tried to escape me.

Suddenly, Kurt turned against his tree and put one arm around the white trunk, putting himself in profile. His hand still stroked his erection, and I wondered who he imagined that tree to be, or if it was only support. I wanted to be that aspen. I wanted to be the one he'd clutch in the throes of passion. I wanted to hold him tightly and feel his breath grow ragged with his approaching climax.

He pumped his cock harder and faster now. I could see him clearly, see how much hard flesh showed beyond his hand on each stroke, and I wanted to touch him there. All I could do was thrust into my own fist and know that I would come soon, but I wanted to hold off until Kurt came. He had to be close. It was so far across the clearing that I couldn't see his face clearly, but it had to be soon. How could he hold onto his come with all the wonderful things he was doing to himself, doing to me?

He froze. It had to be his orgasm, and mine was right there too. The waves of pleasure rolled over me as I climaxed, my come spurting into the undergrowth. The tree I leaned against kept me on my feet. Kurt gripped the aspen, leaning his cheek into the papery bark.

He released his death grip on the tree at last and pulled his clothing back into place. My untanned body probably shone like a beacon in the shadows—I scrambled to yank my utilities back over my ass, and the T-shirt tried to remove one ear when I hauled it over my head again. He was covered and so was I, but the way he had looked naked only moments before burned itself into my memory.

Kurt went to pull the arrows out of the target as if he hadn't given me the most amazing sexual experience of my life. My experiences didn't amount to much, it was true; a few fumblings, gropings, and a blow job that ended before it quite started were about all I ever had, because I hadn't met anyone I wanted to risk so much with. Until now. I simply wished I knew how big of a risk it would be to tell Kurt what I wanted.

One arrow at a time came out of the hay bales as Kurt plucked them from the tight cluster in the center of the target. I watched the way his muscles played under the T-shirt and wondered what to do. Could I go on and keep everything I was thinking, the memory of what I'd seen, off my face? I turned and probably would have made it back to the cabin undetected if I hadn't forgotten the length of the bow. Damned thing was about five and a half feet long, and I managed to whack it smartly into a tree.

Kurt was nearly back to his usual shooting spot; he lifted his head at the sound, and spotted me frantically checking for damage. "Jake? What the hell are you doing to my bow?"

Nothing was busted, except for me. "Sorry." I came out into the meadow, glad enough time had passed that he wouldn't think I'd been spying on him, and glad I had a reason to be embarrassed. When you borrow someone's prized equipment, you have to take care of it.

"Get your butt over here and shoot. You're running out of light." He grinned as I joined him and strung the bow carefully, the way he'd taught me, with the tip braced against a foot and the belly of the bow against my arm. He set the quiver between us, selected an arrow, and turned to shoot without waiting to see what I'd do. His back to me, his face to the target, he released his arrow in a fluid motion.

I tried to do the same, but his *thocked* into the target and mine fell short, though it was on the right path. I picked up another arrow, trying to think what to adjust to get it into the target at all. I'd settle for the gray corners if it would just go in!

We both shot, and his arrow speared the gold center again. At least I managed to get something in the hay bale. Not on the target, but still much better. Sneaking up on the target had taken a humiliating five arrows last time before I even clipped the edge of the hay. Second shot this time. Must be getting better.

Kurt turned to watch me nock the third arrow, and under his eye, I wanted to do better than before. Determined to master the art of the bow, I let the arrow fly at the target, and it imbedded itself in the base of the hay to the left. Consistent, not great. I picked up another arrow.

"Get to shooting stance and stay there, okay?" Kurt examined me critically as I held the position, my right hand near my cheek. "Straighten your wrist. Then you're less likely to introduce torque on the release." He pushed steadily against my wrist, which stuck out, so I straightened it. My skin tingled where he touched me. "Get sighted and release."

This time the arrow hit in the white ring, and if it was the outmost part of the target, it was still on the target! Getting closer.

"Do it again," he told me.

This one went a little wilder, barely clipping the left edge of the hay.

"Come on. Straight wrist, and don't do anything with your fingers besides open them. No fancy twists," Kurt advised me.

I'd been doing a lot more than that with those fingers a little while ago. So had he, and those were the fingers he was touching to mine. To show me what he meant, he took my wrist in one hand, curled my fingers up around an imaginary bowstring, and then straightened them out with his own. "Relax, Jake. Extra movements here and extra tension are going to affect the release." He curled and straightened my hand a few more times as I tried to be relaxed and let my hand open and close without resistance, a nearly impossible task with him standing so close. "Just open easily and naturally."

Oh, that sounded good on a lot of levels, though most of them wouldn't improve my archery skills.

"Try again."

I narrowed my mind down to my right hand, releasing the arrow with the easiest movement I could. This time I clipped the border between the white and black rings, putting the shot two inches closer to the center of the target.

"Better," he commented. "You're getting the hang of it. Most of your upper body is doing the right stuff, but you're consistently shooting to the left." Kurt moved behind me and repositioned my shoulders minutely. "Try this." Yeah, right, after he'd just placed both hands on me, I was going to shoot better. The one time I didn't want him to touch me, he touched me. This arrow went short and right, and would have missed completely had it gone far enough.

"You dropped your elbow that time, which makes a big difference. Think of your arm as being an extension of the arrow, and it all has to point the same direction." Kurt adjusted my stance again, with a touch to my arm that burned like fire. I held the stance as he placed me because I dared not move at all. Now if I could only open my hand naturally, the way he'd been coaching me, the arrow might go where I wanted.

The arrow smacked solidly into the blue, and if it was still several inches away from the center, it was a long way from missing. Not enough to exult over, but it deserved a "Huh."

"All right!" my self-appointed coach proclaimed. "Do it again."

He stepped away to watch me nock my arrow and sight, trying to place every part of me into the same position. I did something differently, because I caught the left edge of the hay again, and he said nothing as I grimly set up the next shot. I would get this right. Into the white this time, and the next arrow was closer yet, almost into the black. Almost. Another half dozen arrows waited in the quiver—bound and determined to get them all onto some part of the target, I selected my next projectile. So, of course I missed the target completely and would have to scout in the grass. "Crap."

"The point of this isn't to get perfect, Jake."

I snapped around in surprise. "It's not?"

He laughed. "No. The point is to get consistent. You have a range with a center. Right now your range is really wide, and your center is several inches off target center. The more you practice, the tighter your range gets, and then you can move your center over. You get a cluster, and your cluster gets smaller."

"Your cluster is about the size of the bull's-eye." I selected another arrow.

"Yeah, but it didn't happen overnight, and I'm using equipment sized for me. Once you get your own bow it will be easier, because your draw should be a little longer than mine. Your arms are longer."

I hadn't thought about that—I had about two inches of height on him.

"Also, if we had our choice of equipment, you'd be doing this part of the learning curve on something lighter, maybe a thirty pound bow. Instead, you're using my short forty-five pound bow. So you're doing better than you think." He smiled at me. If a couple of arrows into the outer rings earned me smiles like that, what would I get for hitting the gold in the center?

Distracted, that's what I would get. This arrow went into the hay, but not the paper. I dragged my mind back onto my mission.

"See? You're pulling into a closer range. I'm going to go back up to the cabin and let you have the rest of the quiver, okay?" He patted me on the shoulder and left. I wouldn't watch him go, because he might turn to see the longing on my face. A pat wasn't enough—it was merely friendly, and I wanted more. If I dwelled on that right now, I'd never hit the damned target again. Sighting down the arrow nocked to the string, I concentrated on my archery, because I was damned well going to master this.

I shot the last few arrows, retrieved them all—even the one that went really wide—and had shot about half of them again when I heard the unmistakable growl of a motorcycle echoing through our clearing. The light was fading enough that I could barely distinguish the black ring from the blue ring of the target, so it was an easy decision to retrieve the arrows and head back to the cabin. Anyone on a bike out here was either aiming for us or totally lost. We'd seen a biker yesterday; this might be the same guy. Maybe he needed directions.

The motor cut off before I came into sight of the cabin. A brief silence followed, suddenly filling with raised voices. I could hear before I could see what was happening, and I didn't like what I heard. I picked up the pace.

NINE

"You gotta have something! Hand it over and nobody gets hurt!" The stranger's words came raggedly. Nope, not directions.

"I told you, we don't have anything. No cash, nothing!" Kurt sounded confident, angry even.

I hurried through the trees. Kurt was equal to most anything, but two of us would be a lot more threatening to anyone stupid enough to say stuff like that. We really didn't have anything up here worth stealing, and we sure didn't have any hoards of money.

Kurt had lit the porch lantern already, and the pool of light showed me a scruffy, gray-haired man in leathers, shaking a fist at Kurt. His bike stood on the far side of him, an old Harley Fat Boy, though he'd taken off the gear that festooned it yesterday, when he'd been a camper and not a threat.

"You gotta have something!" He'd backed Kurt up against the cabin wall. The dude was seriously big. Half a head taller than Kurt and fat, but under the layer of padding lay some muscle, which he used to throw Kurt against the wall and keep him pinned there. The guy reached for something at his side, and then he brandished a knife toward Kurt's face.

Shit!

"Come on, fork it over, pretty boy, and you can stay pretty." He held the tip of the knife right below Kurt's eye. "You gotta have something, a cell phone or anything! I need it!" Both pitch and volume rose as he shook Kurt, who tipped his head back away from the blade. "Now, damn it!"

Kurt's eyes were wide as he looked at the knife so close to his cheek. "About the only thing is some binoculars!"

I could not believe this shithead had pulled a weapon on Kurt! But if the biker was armed, so was I.

With an arrow nocked, I stepped out of the trees and in my deepest, most threatening voice snarled, "Let him go and get the hell out of here!" I aimed carefully. At a range shorter by half than where I'd been practicing, my arrow would hit.

Despite the dire situation, a strange calm settled over me. Blackness took my peripheral vision and the world narrowed down to me, Kurt, and an ugly bastard who'd better get the hell away from my partner. I couldn't give a rat's ass about my own safety in that moment, but if that fucker drew one drop of Kurt's blood....

The biker turned to me, taking a step backward. Hoping that the varnish would catch the light, I swung the bow in a tiny arc, wanting him to see his armed opponent. At least he'd taken the knife away from Kurt's face, though he still had a fistful of green T-shirt.

Kurt's eyes got even wider, which I could understand because I tended to shoot to the left, and there he was, on the left side of my range. He said nothing about that, of course, but narrowed his eyes thoughtfully, like Biker Boy was in as much danger as if Kurt were the one holding the bow. "If I were you, man, I'd get while the getting was good." Even in his fear he made one hell of an actor, and if I didn't see the trembling in his fingers, I might have thought him cool and collected.

"Brave little men," the biker sneered. "I ain't going no damned where without some money or something I can hock! Where's your first aid kit? You got any drugs in there? I bet you do." He started to turn back to Kurt. I let the arrow fly. It swished behind him and struck. I had another arrow on the bow string before the metallic clang stopped echoing. He swiveled around madly, trying to find where the arrow went.

"You fucker! You shot my hog!" He threw Kurt to one side and fisted his hands, bellowing. Kurt wisely scrambled toward me before the guy realized he'd both lost his hostage and had an arrow sticking out of his gas tank.

"You shot my fucking bike!" He swung back toward me, as angry as a bee-stung bear. I aimed again. Kurt had ducked around behind me, but the tug on the quiver at my waist told me he was acquiring a weapon of his own without fouling my shot. Now he stood beside me with an arrow in each hand.

I laughed, intentionally throwing in all the evil I could muster, hoping it would mask my surprise at nailing that particular target on the first shot. "Next one goes into you, shithead." If he rushed us, I could get an arrow into that big belly at point blank range, no problem. While I'd never hurt anyone deliberately before, first time for everything.

He paused at the promise and looked back at his bike. In the light of the lantern, the end of the twenty-eight inch arrow with its white and green fletching could clearly be seen. The hydrocarbon tang of gasoline permeated the air. Kurt and I were well away from the pool of light; now we were a threat in the near dark.

"Better leave while you still have some gas to do it with,

dude," Kurt remarked mildly. "We don't have anything you want, and we have a lot you don't. I reckon the Chief ought to be coming up the road any minute now, making his evening rounds." Damn, how easily the lie slipped off Kurt's tongue.

We could have melted back into the woods, but that would have looked like running away and might have given this guy ideas about trashing our place to get even. And Kurt's bluff said we were waiting for the non-existent cavalry to arrive. Better to look and sound dangerous, I thought, holding the bow at the ready. Besides, I almost itched to shoot again: how dare this asshole threaten my partner! "Get on your bike, head it down the road, and get your sorry ass out of here. Now. While you still can."

It cost the guy something to get on his bike and fire up the engine, I could tell. Nobody would want to be run off an easy target by a guy with a medieval weapon. He looked at the bike, and he looked at us, and he must have decided that the pickings were too slim to be worth getting skewered over. His desperation might lead him to come back later for revenge, but we'd just have to see. Being alone in the woods meant doing without 911, cops, and sirens, but we weren't helpless—far from it.

"God damn you little shits!" He bent to examine the tank, his butt making a target broad enough I was sure I could hit it, even with the shakes threatening to set in. The temptation to try passed when he jumped aboard. He fired up the engine, then kicked the gearshift without trying to pull out the arrow. He roared off, tires scrabbling for purchase on the rutted dirt track, still screaming anger that featured the word "fuck" prominently. Engine sounds dwindled into the distance, but one last "Asshole!" came back over his shoulder.

A huge sigh of relief made me turn around. "At least Motorcycle Boy is unlikely to sneak up on us," Kurt observed at last.

He stowed his two arrows back in the quiver—the soft, raspy, sliding sound they made seemed suddenly loud.

Slightly shaky now, I stood down and let the bow return to rest without releasing the arrow. "Yeah. He doesn't really strike me as the type up for a long hike in the woods." I stowed my arrow and looked at the bow, which I hadn't unstrung when I decided to come investigate—and a good thing, too. "Are you okay?" I was probably violating the guy code for even asking, but hell, Kurt had just had a knife pulled on him.

"Yeah, fine." He patted my shoulder again and let his hand rest a fraction of a second before he punched me gently. "Glad you showed up when you did, though. The paperwork on the binoculars would have been a bitch to fill out." He spoke lightly, but the slight tension around his eyes belied his nonchalance.

He had to be hiding his relief just as I was hiding mine. I pushed it to the back of my mind when what I really wanted to hold him tightly, examine him all over for injuries, and then kiss him for being all right. "Yeah, those triplicate forms suck, don't they? You'd get writer's cramp."

"Your aim got awfully good when it was you faced with triplicate forms." He smacked my arm in comradely fashion. "Glad you didn't misplace me."

Guess my aim had been good enough to run Biker Boy off, but it wasn't anywhere near as good as Kurt thought. I wasn't going to enlighten him.

I went to stow the now-unstrung bow on its hook in the cabin, but I did put the compound bow that was always at the ready near the door. Kurt headed to the truck. I guessed he intended to radio the incident in to headquarters. There wasn't much else we could do besides hope this guy wouldn't stumble onto any of the innocents on the mountain tonight. The Scouts would be farther off the beaten path than the biker seemed likely to go, and who knew about the pair in the red RAV4? With luck, he'd have enough fuel to get to Meeker, where he'd either get picked up or keep going.

"The Chief promised to pass it on to the sheriff," Kurt reported as he came back to the cabin, carrying the lantern in from the porch. "I called Max, too. Biker Boy might think he could take on the folks at the lodge."

"Whoa, that would be a bad idea." Max was a mild-looking man, but he gave off a very practical kind of vibe. With all the wildlife prowling around, I had no doubt he kept quite an arsenal.

"Yeah. Max would shoot first, park the bike next to the diesel generator, and haul the body off into the woods on horseback. I'd have to write him a citation for feeding the bears." He chuckled, the sound getting lost in the thud of his boots when he kicked them off to get ready for bed. We rose and set with the sun, pretty much, and dawn never failed to bring more work. I tried not to follow him with my eyes as he peeled down to skivvies and slipped into his sleeping bag, making the cot squeak under his weight. I did the same, getting into the bag on my own narrow camp cot. He doused the lantern and said goodnight. All was quiet except for the thousand lonely frogs and crickets. The owl hooted from the distant trees, warning the forest that predators stalked the night. I already knew.

We lay silently for a long time, and then I heard him turn over. "Jake?" he asked softly, his voice scarcely above a whisper.

"Yeah?" I allowed myself a second's fantasy that he was going to ask to join me.

"Thanks." He turned over in the cot again.

I would have said yes. "You'd have done the same for me."

"I would, but still…." He'd probably have done it better too.

There wasn't anything to say other than, "It's okay."

We lay in silence again, and eventually Kurt's breathing took on that soft, regular rhythm of sleep. I lay awake a while longer, listening to him and listening for the roar of a Harley in the night.

TEN

Kurt leaped out of bed, yodeling "Whoo hoo! We're going to town today!" as he bounced around getting dressed. We'd been good on the casual nudity that naturally happens when two people share a sixteen by sixteen foot cabin, but that was before my jury-rigged obliviousness to him had shattered. I caught a flash of skin before he dove all the way into a relatively clean shirt. I had to pull the sleeping bag up over my head, hoping he'd dress as quickly as he'd peeled off last night.

"People who are too cheerful in the morning get hurt," I warned from my cocoon, grouchy from lack of sleep. From my guesstimate, I'd lain awake until somewhere around 3:00 a.m. Apparently he'd forgotten all about out little adventure from the night before.

"Come on, you aren't excited by the thought of clean clothes and fresh food and a hot shower with real soap?" He rattled off the main delights of a trip to town. "Especially the food?"

"Well, of course, but not to the point of singing." I poked

my nose out of the sleeping bag; a good glare required eye contact.

"I sincerely hope nothing excites you to the point of singing," he said with a laugh, "since your voice would scare the ravens right out of the trees."

"Thanks a lot," I grumbled. "Maybe I should have given our visitor last night a few rousing verses of 'Waltzing Matilda'." I decided it was safe enough to get up and get dressed. The sight of Kurt shoving his last few T-shirts into the laundry bag shouldn't arouse me.

"Nah, 'Kumbayah' would have been worse—or better, as the case may be." He shook his sleeping bag out to straighten it, as he did every morning, though I never bothered. A used sock tumbled out. He squatted to pick it up and wrinkled his nose at its rancid mate that he pulled out from under the cot. "Phew."

"Too bad you couldn't have waved that sock at him. It would have done the trick." I nudged him off balance with my foot as I passed; he toppled onto one knee with a thud.

"Ow. For that you make breakfast."

"Hah. Anything I make, you have to eat." We'd gotten used to giving each other a certain amount of crap over the last few weeks. It felt nice and normal. I still scrambled into my clothing, because he was turning around to look at me, and I didn't think I could do normal to the point of not reacting.

"Even you couldn't wreck peanut butter and jelly sandwiches and canned peaches."

"That's really all that's left in the bear box?" There wasn't even a lot of peanut butter. I threw my last clean clothes on the cot and finished stuffing the dirty ones into the bag. Tossing my laundry bag into the back seat of the Toyota on the way to the box that served as our pantry, I tried to remember if the bear had left us anything else. There really had to be a better way to store food securely than leaving everything in a metal safe to bake in the sun.

Such were my thoughts as I fetched the last of the bread and other things and slapped some sandwiches together. Kurt came back from throwing his laundry bag into the Toyota and started to open the peaches. Good old can opener. "Let's just slurp the peaches straight from the can," he suggested. "Speed the washing up?"

"Works for me!" It would get us on the road thirty seconds faster, and I watched Kurt from the corner of my eye as he tipped the can up to get his share of the fruit. A dribble of juice ran down the corner of his mouth. I was tempted to lick it away, but he swiped his arm across his face before I could do anything stupid.

We rattled up the dirt road toward town in my elderly Toyota. We'd fill it up with supplies and folded clothes, but right now it was us and the laundry. No air conditioning—my student budget hadn't permitted it—so we rolled down the windows and didn't try to talk until we got to pavement. Dust from the road flew in through the open windows to mix with the stench of sweaty clothing as we rattled down the washboard road, temporarily drowning out the calls of the meadowlarks and ravens.

"You're really wearing that to town?" Kurt eyed my hat. He adjusted the blue jay feathers in the band of his own ranger-standard flat-brim.

"I like this hat. It keeps the rain off my head." The vibrations made it bounce around, so I pulled it down more tightly over my brow.

"We haven't had rain in weeks and we need some. It would make our job easier." Kurt looked upward, as if he could generate a storm from the wanting. "Maybe if you took the hat off you could tease the clouds into a few drops. You know, like it always rains after you wash your car. Or maybe we could wash the car in town. Although we're never going to get it to be anything but dirt-colored."

I chose not to answer that, mostly because "dirt-colored" was the kindest term he'd applied to the crudmobile thus far. "So, first stop is headquarters or the laundromat?" I asked once town was in sight. Meeker, population twenty-two hundred, boasted the finest washing machines in the county.

"Let's hit HQ first. Then we can shower and shave." His chin, like my own, sported a two-day growth of stubble. Another day or two and we'd look fashionable, but today we looked scruffy. Kurt's whiskers were slightly darker blond than his hair, but much lighter than my own coffee-grounds brown.

"Crap, I forgot to grab my clean clothes and stuff!" I could have struck my own forehead with dismay, except for wanting both hands to drive. I'd laid them out on top of the sleeping bag and hadn't checked again after Kurt said he loaded the car.

"I did get them off the cot, and you can use my dopp kit," Kurt offered, and I could hear, if not see, the twinkle in his eye. "But that means I get first shower!"

"Sure," I said with relief as I pulled into the drive in front of HQ, which doubled as the Chief's home. The curbs were no longer cluttered with rangers' personal vehicles, and the brick house looked much larger for not having a crowd spilling out of it. We entered what used to be the living room, the walls covered in maps, the big desk strewn with papers, and a radio base station taking up one corner of the table pushed up against the long wall. A pressure gauge from some team's tanker lay in pieces on the table, tools nearby. "Command central" smelled more like a bakery than an office.

"Hi, boys!" called Mrs. Chief from the rear of the house.

"Your timing is perfect. The brownies are still hot out of the oven." She came up the hallway from the kitchen in a draft of chocolate, which smelled even better than the banana bread she'd made last week, or the sugar cookies the week before.

"You take such good care of us!" Kurt hugged the slightly graying, fifty-something woman, who laughed and hugged him back. "Will you be my mother?"

"No adoptions finalized until after the end of your third season, dear, and I'll still make you do your own laundry," she warned as she turned and took my hand.

"Third season?" I whimpered, sniffing the wonderful aroma.

"Yes. It takes that long to housebreak rangers, though Rich and Abigail did scrub the bathroom yesterday. They're coming along beautifully." She smiled with satisfaction.

"Maybe you can teach Kurt to pick up his socks," I suggested, thinking back to the crusty thing he'd extracted from under the cot.

That got me a small kiss to the cheek, though she had to reach to get me. "Pick up your socks, Kurt," she said, and he rolled his eyes. "Now, do you want milk or coffee with the brownies?"

What a choice to have to make. We hadn't seen either fresh milk or decent coffee in a week. Iced tea at the lodge had been the liquid indulgence there.

"Both," she went on—she must have divined the dilemma. "Growing boys need their milk. Harold will be back in a moment." I had to think who Harold was: no one ever referred to him as anything but "Chief."

Grown boys who had no access to fresh baked things most of the week made the plate of brownies disappear in nearly record time, washed down with a big pot of coffee and big glasses of milk. I never appreciated such things when they were readily available, and now that they were a once-a-week treat, they tasted all the sweeter. I'd just finished my third cup of coffee and we were both eyeing the last two brownies, which we really should save for the Chief, when he came in.

"Glad to see you, boys. In fact, the sheriff will be glad to see you, too." We stared at him, before memory kicked in. "He wants to talk about your incident last night. That man didn't steal anything or harm either of you, did he?"

"No, he didn't, though if Jake hadn't turned up when he did, I might have needed a lot of stitches." Kurt's eyes turned cloudy, and I imagined he was seeing that knife at close range in his mind. He'd yukked it up so well this morning that I'd nearly forgotten the terror in his eyes the night before. Seemed my partner liked to put on an "I am a rock" act. "He wanted hockable stuff or cash. Guess he was thinking of his next fix. Or his next drink." Kurt visibly threw off his thoughts. "He kinda reeked of stale booze, and I don't think he'd had a bath this month."

I missed that joy last night. The dripping gasoline had shut my nose down before I walked through any stink Biker Boy left behind.

"The most valuable thing in the cabin wouldn't have done a thing for him, though."

"What's that?" asked Mrs. Chief, as she poured coffee into her husband's cup and again into mine. I would have picked the binoculars or the two-way radio.

"The can opener, of course," Kurt said blandly and snickered at us for snorting coffee. You'd think he hadn't stared at the tip of a knife at close range last night.

Once the Chief stopped laughing, he went back to business. Apparently, he wasn't wise to Kurt's act. "Who's going to give report?"

"I am," I said. Since I was the less experienced member of the team, I'd do it and learn something in the process. Kurt must have thought I could handle it alone, or that Chief could help me, because he announced that he'd hit the shower.

"I'll grab your stuff, too, Jake," he said, and soon he'd disappeared into the back of the house.

As I talked with the Chief, pushing pins into maps and discussing how conditions were changing, I became uncomfortably aware of pressure in my bladder. All that good coffee demanded to be recycled. Once I'd become aware of that, I realized that the background hum came from the pipes. Kurt was in the shower.

Running water: what a bad thought for right now. Kurt naked in the running water: worse thought for right now. If I got hard, I at least wouldn't piss myself, but I would surely embarrass myself. Oh hell, I was doomed to embarrass myself one way or another.

Last week, before my façade cracked, I would have casually strolled to the bathroom and taken care of the problem, whether or not Kurt showered a few feet away. Now, with him naked on the other side of a clear curtain, I couldn't just whip it out and whizz. The pressure inside grew as I agonized.

I tried to keep my mind on the Chief's instructions, but the internal signals were slowly driving me crazy. Kurt might look if I went in. Kurt might not look—he might ignore me. That would be worse. Kurt might look and be repulsed; that would be a lot worse. Kurt might look and like it. That would be way worse, because thinking about that would cause an unmistakable bulge with the Chief sitting close enough to see. I tried to focus on moisture content and rainfall reports.

My concentration waned, what with part of me tuned to the sound of the shower. Any minute now I'd lose control. I prayed for the water to stop running and that I could wait the few more minutes Kurt would need to get dressed and out of the bathroom. *Please, please, please, please, please.* I squirmed and wriggled in my seat: "comfortable" didn't stand a chance in hell. Not with the thoughts spinning around my brain.

My internal conflict must have been showing, because the Chief looked at me with concern, right about the time the water stopped. "Are you okay, son?"

"Yeah, it's nothing." I counted the seconds, trying to think how long it would take Kurt to dress. Praying that he'd already done everything in the sink that he needed to, because things were getting desperate. "We had a strike here, last week, but it just smoldered a little." I pointed to the map. "Moisture levels were good. It took us about twenty minutes to deal with it."

The Chief lifted one brow, and I realized I'd already said that once. Trying and failing to find an intelligent comment, I stuttered, and then, oh glory be, I heard the bathroom door open. "Excuse me, sir!" I bolted from the room and toward the back of the house surprising Kurt, who was halfway out of the bathroom, chased by a cloud of steam. I pushed past him and slammed the door behind me. I fumbled my fly open in the nick of time, milliseconds before the flood started. Sweet relief, and then Kurt's voice floated in from the hallway.

The closed door didn't keep me from hearing him say, "You could have just come on in."

Oh hell no, I couldn't.

ELEVEN

I shut my eyes. Kurt went on to say, "Everything's in there, you might as well take care of business while you're at it. I'll go finish with the Chief."

Maybe after that I could get back under control. The dopp kit sat open on the counter next to a pile of fresh clothing. One last folded towel sat on the wire rack, so I had everything I needed. My pants were already open, a situation that seemed to be all too frequent these days. I hoped Kurt had left some hot water, because I wasn't going to try for the cold shower this time. Dirty clothing hit the floor, and I stepped into the spray.

A washcloth and a cold lake are pretty good for getting clean; soap isn't the necessity Dr. Bonner would have you believe. A lot of scrubbing will do it without polluting the lake, but it isn't the same as a hot shower. Even the camp shower, which lets you wet yourself with sun-warmed water, doesn't come close. I rubbed shampoo into my short brown hair, wondering if I needed to get it cut to keep it manageable for our conditions. Kurt still looked okay, so I could probably go another week or two. I scraped my chin after my whiskers had a chance to soften in the moist air and shaving cream. I'd smell like him now; I didn't normally use his brand.

That thought and my soapy hands hardened up my cock, and while I wasn't alone in the house, it was as private as I could have hoped for. I soaped my body, letting my mind run free. I envisioned Kurt washing me, and then I had to drop to my knees in the tub.

The water poured on my head as I grasped my engorged shaft and stroked. The hot water would run out—and so would our hosts' patience. I didn't try to slow anything. This time I imagined every detail I could, but it all came down to sweet touching on my cock, which stuck far out from my body. I was big, and Kurt had looked sizable. I imagined holding one of us in each hand and then went on to imagining how he would put his mouth over the head of my cock. He'd have to spread his lips to accommodate my shaft, because it expanded to a wider girth a short way below the head. I pumped and then put the other hand, still soapy, under my balls and played with them under the skin. I did everything I loved, everything I knew would make me come quickly, as I arched my back and caught the water in my face. I looked down over my chest and saw how my cock stood out clearly, reddish against the white tub, my thighs framing my busy hand, and saw Kurt's face again. I wanted to dwell on the fantasy of him putting his mouth over my shaft once more, but the image had the punch to drive me over the edge, and I shot milky come toward the drain.

When I staggered to my feet and rinsed, knees still slightly shaky, the hot water started running out. Playing with myself had served its purpose, and now I could be calm enough to go face everyone. I snatched up the last towel, scrubbed it over my wondrously grime-free skin. I would grab the rest out of the hamper to launder with our things. And now for some really clean clothes. Clean underwear, a shirt that hadn't already had a day out in the truck, and pants without dirt on the knees. Socks that didn't walk on their own. Kurt had brought my stuff in, and I hunted for the first layer.

Shit. I could have sworn I put underwear in the stack back in the cabin. It should have been under the shirt and on top of the utility pants. With the socks. I held up the socks in disbelief, as if they might have eaten the underwear, but no, they concealed nothing, and shaking the pants out didn't make any welcome cotton bundles fall to the floor. Putting the others back on was out of the question. Going commando was equally out of the question. Asking to borrow a pair from the Chief was *really* out of the question.

I chose the least of the three evils, opting to go commando. I slid gingerly into the green denim utilities, grateful for the loose fit. Great. I'd be walking around Meeker flapping free in there. I took a really deep breath and wondered if my underwear lay on the floor in the hallway, ready to be found by Mrs. Chief. Okay, make that four evils.

I took the armful of towels and clothing out to the car after scanning the floor for escaped BVDs. The denim chafed. I should have stuffed the damned underwear into one of the many pockets on the pants. I should have seen to loading my own stuff. I was going to have to ignore the feeling of freedom where normally cotton supported my package. I couldn't even joke about it to Kurt, which I might have done before, to alleviate my discomfort. This could be a really long day.

TWELVE

There were enough machines free in the laundromat that we could shove everything in at the same time. The underwear that flew into the washer might as well have been on Mars for all the good they did me, though it might be different in an hour or so. Kurt shook detergent on top of the clothing and handed the box to me.

"Do you know where the red sock is?" he asked innocently.

"What red sock?" I growled. This day had enough irritations already. "I don't wear red socks." Pink whites would really be the last straw.

"Neither do I. Just checking." He hauled the box of detergent back out to the car. Great. Now I'd be wondering if someone had left a red sock behind from the last load before mine. So the girl with an overflowing basket of clothes behind me came as a complete surprise. I turned into her, knocking her sprawling and her laundry flying, so I had to help pick everything up and apologize. I don't know whose face went redder, hers or mine, but I managed to escape before she asked me anything like my name or which section I patrolled.

Kurt was leaning against the front fender of my car, grinning like a fool when I came out and slammed into the driver's seat.

"A script writer couldn't have done a better 'meet cute' scene," he suggested through the open window. I growled something about how "meet cute" sucked.

"Did she have lacy undies?" he pursued. My hand itched. If I checked, it would have a pink lacy rash, I just knew it.

"This would be a nice time to shut up, Kurt." Undies were a sore subject at that moment, and I wasn't about to discuss this new medical problem. If Kurt asked, I'd tell him I'd found a patch of poison ivy.

"Then let's go to the library next. I'll have to be quiet there." Kurt made no move to get in the car. I glared at him. "Or if you have something else to do, I'll walk over. It's about two blocks."

In downtown Meeker, very little was more than two blocks away. I got out of the car, feeling doubly foolish for forgetting everything wasn't in driving distance, like back home in the suburbs of Detroit. "Let's go. You know where it is. You lead." I waved him on, risking a quick check on my hand. No rash.

Two blocks was enough for me to see that Kurt had been incorporated into the fabric of the town. People waved, and a few called him by name. He waved back and tipped his hat to the women. A small boy raced past on a bike with training wheels, screaming, "Hi, Kurt!"

"Hi, Tiger!" he yelled back.

"You know everyone?" I waved too, to be friendly.

"Keep waving, and you'll know everybody soon. There aren't that many people here. You can call all the kids 'Tiger', and they'll answer to it." He pushed open the door to the library, a tiny building that housed one of the best aspects of civilization: books.

The librarian stood up at his wave and came to speak softly with us. "Do you need the computer again, Kurt?"

"Yes, please, Mrs. Wood." He followed her behind the desk and sat to type. I followed, too, wondering what he planned.

"I'm going to update my blog, Jake. One of these days"—here he looked up at me with a twinkle—"it's going to pay off. Right now the revenues are about thirty-five cents a month." He typed in a password, and scenes of the Colorado mountains that we patrolled gave way to administrative screens. "Maybe a picture or two of you in there will boost revenues to forty cents."

"Funny." I watched the screen and his tapping fingers assembling a post.

"Just going to put in something about the fire. It'll take me a few minutes." Kurt shooed me away. "Go find a book."

I wandered the stacks, wondering what sort of book would have the answers in it that I really needed. Probably nothing the public library stocked—I didn't expect to find *How to Seduce the Straight Guy and Make Him Like It* on the shelves. I might be better off looking for *Saltpeter: Its Uses and Preparation*. A history of the area looked interesting, and I picked up a collection of short stories that would probably not get opened, but it made Mrs. Wood happy. I began to see what Kurt meant about getting to know everyone.

"Done, Jake." Kurt rose from the computer. "We can go find some groceries now."

He headed toward the car when we came back to the main street, but I headed the other way, because what I wanted was on the next block. I let him figure it out and catch up to me. "Not ready for 'meet cute' phase two? Or do you plan to wheel the groceries four blocks back to the laundry?"

"No and no. You'll see."

He followed me when I turned toward the hardware store. "We aren't going to get much Spam here. Or should I shut up again?"

Actually, this time I wanted to gloat. "I am not eating that again if at all possible. I am not eating powdered eggs. I am not drinking powdered milk. Even in coffee." Pausing with my hand on the door, I reeled off what else I wanted. "I am going to eat vegetation every day of the week, and I am going to have a real fried egg six days from now. Fried in butter, I tell you."

He looked at me in shock. "You're quitting the Forest Service?"

I roared. I couldn't help it. I threw my head back and howled with laughter. Every cranky thought fled, every irritation with missing underwear and someone else's razor evaporated. Even the upcoming interview with the sheriff got lost in the hilarity of the conclusion he'd just jumped to. The more I laughed, the more he relaxed, and pretty soon he was smiling again, too, and even chuckling.

"I take it that's a 'no'."

"Kurt, your Uncle Jake is a genius. I'm not quitting. I'm not even moving to a desk job in town." The flash of relief that passed over his face turned to open curiosity before I was quite sure I'd seen it. "I am going to take advantage of a natural feature to improve our quality of life. Come with me and marvel at my brilliance." I wouldn't say anything else; I went into the hardware store, with Kurt trailing behind, and selected the things I'd decided we needed.

Into the cart went a ninety-five quart plastic container, some long bungee cords, one hundred feet of nylon rope, a pulley, and a box of one-gallon zipper bags, which I could have probably bought at the grocery store, but I wanted to show a complete set up. "Behold, young Kurt, a wilderness refrigerator." I waved theatrically at my selections.

"Uh, right." He didn't appear convinced.

"Dear me, never show a fool a half job." I made a *tsk tsk* noise. I might have been less dramatic, but smarting over the "red sock" and "meet cute" jokes made me want to return the favor. "We still need to install the cooling unit. Or rather, install our new fridge in the cooling unit." Light began to dawn—his face showed his understanding. "Kurt, that is one damned cold lake. We might as well use it."

We laughed like loons all the way to the grocery store, making lists of things we wanted to get and could never reasonably take with us before.

"Mayonnaise! Eggs!" I shouted.

"Hamburgers!" Kurt dreamed out loud. "Cheese!"

"Butter!" we breathed in unison.

"Milk," Kurt practically moaned. "The cereal can live in the bear box."

"Tuna fish!"

"You want something that comes in a can? I thought we were done with cans." Kurt sounded puzzled.

"Not done with cans, just not dependent on cans like before. Tuna will taste a helluva lot better with mayonnaise." I could hardly wait to taste it. "We can eat like normal people if we can keep some things cold."

Kurt tweaked my Aussie hat down. "Vegemite?"

"If they stock it, you're going to eat it, smartass."

Kurt was probably safe, but he made a gagging noise anyway.

We pushed the cart through the aisles at the market, loading it with things we'd never bought in more than one-day quantities. The eggs made me smile; to hell with the powdered crap. A second dozen joined the first. Frozen hamburger patties went with buns, and tomatoes got placed carefully on top of the cereal boxes.

Kurt followed me down an aisle of cake mixes and chocolate chips. "Don't get ahead of yourself, Jake. We still can't bake on a propane stove."

"I do know how to do it with a Dutch oven and a fire, but we aren't home long enough to get it started and still eat before midnight. But we can have French toast for breakfast!" I found a ten-pound bag of flour that would go in the bear box and another bag of brown sugar to replace what the bear had stolen.

"I can even make that, smartass." Kurt put bottles of cooking oil and syrup in the cart.

"Good. You're in charge of breakfast tomorrow. Don't forget the baking soda." I trundled away to the dairy section to examine the milk containers. Surely one sort wouldn't need to be bagged or kept upright.

"Catch any crocodiles yet?" Lindy the checkout girl had decided to take a less full-on approach since she'd seen the whites of my eyes show, I supposed.

"Something of a crocodile shortage around these parts, ma'am." I tipped my hat to her. "G'day."

"Ask him to say 'Crikey!'" Kurt suggested as he put groceries on the conveyor belt.

"Yeah! Say 'Crikey'!" She giggled as she swiped the milk over the scanner and bagged it.

"I like my Aussie hat, and I am not saying 'Crikey'!" I set the lettuce and tomatoes down for her to scan.

"You just did!" they chorused.

"Agh!" I yanked my hat off and smacked Kurt across the arm with it. "Keep that up and I'll sing every last verse of

'Waltzing Matilda' on the way back to the cabin!" I parked my bushranger back on my head with a dashing tilt.

"No! No!" Kurt howled in mock horror. At least, I think it was mock horror.

"Gee, I think you should sing it at the Flat Tops Lounge. It's karaoke night. Want to?" The cashier, distracted by trying to entice me, scanned the butter, missed, and had to rescan. She was persistent, I'll give her that, but we'd both been saying, "No thanks," since that first shopping trip.

"Want to see how fast they throw me out for being the worst karaoke singer they've ever heard?" I wasn't really kidding, and Kurt wasn't helping by putting his hands over his ears and shaking his head with anticipated pain, mouthing, "No, no, no, no."

"We could go bowling instead," she offered. "Kurt, Tanya might be there. She mentioned that great spare you picked up last year. I could call her..." She tilted her head to look up through her lashes, making me glad I didn't have to evade her every day.

"We've got a technical problem. We need to get the chow back home before anything spoils," Kurt told her as he put the eggs down tenderly.

She scanned them, disappointed. "I was wondering. This doesn't look like normal ranger rations."

"No, genius here figured out how to keep stuff cold!" Kurt loaded the conveyor with the last perishables.

"All right!" Her words got drowned out in the scanner's beeping, but her smile was wide enough to see from outer space. "So, which one of you is the chef?"

"He is!" we said together.

She laughed. "Maybe Tanya and I should come out and fix

dinner for you." Apparently she and her archrival had divided us up between them and now they could hunt in pairs.

"That's sweet of you, but we need to learn how to do it." Kurt counted out bills into her hand.

"Then we'll give you a week or two to practice and you can cook dinner for us!" Blue eyes batted behind her round glasses.

"Two weeks might not be enough to improve our bachelor cooking into edibility. Better not risk it." I had to admire how he turned "no" into something she could accept with a smile, even though I could feel her eyes on our backs as we hauled our prizes to the Toyota. I was relieved he turned her down. She'd brushed my hand with hers while loading the last bag into the cart. Lindy in a less public place might be a lot harder to avoid.

Back at the laundromat, I gazed wistfully at my sopping wet underwear, which travelled from washer to dryer without landing on me. They could spin around and get wearable while we went to talk to the sheriff. I'd been ignoring my commando state as best I could, though I think Lindy might have noticed. She certainly spent enough time staring at that part of my anatomy. With luck, the sheriff wouldn't.

We'd been told to come by the office around noon, since the sheriff would be back by then. That made me a little queasy because I didn't like thinking about last night and how close Kurt had come to getting hurt. I hadn't shared something about the way the whole thing had gone down—I didn't really want to tell him. Maybe that aspect of it wouldn't come up.

"Hello, men." I'd met the sheriff before, during orientation, and hadn't had reason to talk to him since. Tall and lanky, with a uniform so crisp that it probably saluted him every morning, he was the epitome of The Law. It was an elective office in this county, but Michael Dodd had a reputation for taking the job seriously. "Heard you had a spot of trouble last night."

"Nothing we couldn't handle, sir. No bloodshed." We told the story of the encounter again, taking turns adding details.

"Would you recognize the man if you saw him again?" the Sheriff asked. He led us to a door that had a hand-lettered sign saying "Pokey" and opened it, revealing two cells. One was empty, but the other made any question of recognition a moot point. Harley Boy looked up and snarled.

"Should have cut you fuckers up while I had the chance, you sonofabitch, cheap-ass bastards...." He rattled the bars of his cell, making me grateful they were between him and us—he looked smaller in the light, but angrier, more desperate, as he dragged himself to his feet, hand over hand. "Get over here. I'll fix you...."

The sheriff shut the door again. "That answers that. Old Desperado won't be around again. We caught him trying to break into the Gaston house in the early hours this morning. We could keep him on that, or on menacing you two, but I think we'll let him be a guest of the county until someone comes up from Denver and collects him. They want him for just about everything you can think of down there."

"Glad someone wants him. We sure don't." Kurt looked grimly satisfied at this news.

"Good job on scaring him off instead of hurting him, Jake. Keeps the paperwork down. Ummm... you boys missing something?" He reached into his desk drawer to extract Kurt's arrow. "I think I'd keep that one, if I were you." Sheriff Dodd passed the arrow to Kurt and dismissed us with a handshake. I burned with shame at the praise, knowing I didn't deserve it, and I let Kurt lead the conversation on the way back to the laundry. Somehow I couldn't think of anything worthwhile to say.

THIRTEEN

The clothes were dry, but the underwear were no closer to being on me than they had been while wet. Where could I go to put them on? The laundromat's bathroom sported a hand-lettered "Out of order" sign and a padlock on the door. I folded them with longing and placed them in the bag with regret. I was moving around in there, chafing, and it was about to get embarrassing as Kurt bent into the dryer, retrieving another armload of clothing. His ass stuck out invitingly, green fabric stretched tight over his buttocks. As I looked away, I noticed the girl whose things I'd knocked over admiring the view too.

"Hey, guys, I think one of you left this in the washer." She came over with a wad of damp, blue fabric, which she snapped out to transform into a pair of Kurt's underwear. She lifted her shoulders to stand up very straight, chest thrust out like a robin redbreast.

"Thanks." Kurt reached for them without making eye contact, but she pulled back a trifle.

"Kind of nice to know it isn't ranger green all the way to your skin." She flipped her long, blond hair back over her shoulder. "Your stuff is pretty much dry. I've got a load going into the dryer. Want me to throw them in? We could go over to the coffee shop and have some pie while the machine's going." Her smile included me in the invitation, as if handling laundry was a social introduction.

I snapped a towel into straightness, irritated with her, yet knowing that Kurt did attract that kind of attention—this was hardly the first time, even today.

"They can air dry, thanks. May I have them back? I don't usually let strangers handle my underwear." He held out his hand again.

"I'm Dawn. Now I'm not a stranger." She swung the underwear by the elastic on one finger. "Really, they can dry with my things."

"Not with a car full of foods that have a long way to go to get to the fridge, and we still need to build the fridge." He looked at her cajolingly. "Please, Dawn?"

If he worked this right, he could have dry underwear, a piece of pie, and probably a piece of Dawn. I just didn't want to hear him work his charm on her, but he wasn't really laying it on, either.

"We should chill the eggs before we can hear the salmonella dividing in there," I put in, as I folded the last of Mrs. Chief's ranger towels. Dawn handed over the underwear, shoulders slumping, and went back to throwing things from the washer to the dryer.

We did move the car this time because of the laundry and groceries. Dropping off the towels would be our last stop in town, and I could do a small task to complete our wilderness fridge. The Chief led me back to the garage with the ninety-five-quart container in hand. Kurt ducked into the house with the stack of clean towels. "What size bit do you want?" the Chief asked, pulling his power drill off the shelf.

I'd thought about weight and water when I stowed the plastic box in the back seat. "Quarter inch or larger, if you have it." He handed me a half-inch masonry bit, which I chucked into the drill, and then I squeezed off an experimental burst of electricity.

"That container would weigh about what you do, if it were full," the Chief said, brow wrinkled. "You'd need to drain it to lift it at all."

"I might need to do a proper block and tackle anyway." I started a series of holes across the sides, wondering how many holes it would take to fatally weaken the bottom. "But this should get it down to not much more than the weight of the food."

"Let me know how it works," said the Chief, as he left me to the scream of the drill. "I have a feeling the other rangers will be mighty interested if you boys manage to pull this off. They'll all want a box of their own."

We cleared the edge of town before Kurt brought up the girls. "Maybe I shouldn't have been making your decisions for you back there, Jake. I'm sorry if I cramped your style or anything."

"Didn't notice you making any decisions I disagreed with." At this point, I still wasn't sure what he was talking about.

"All you'd need to do is crook your finger at Lindy, and she'd come running. Or Dawn. I don't think she'd care which one of us she got her hands on, and you've already seen her underwear." He tipped the seat back down a bit and stretched out.

I passed a stock truck before I answered that. "No kidding.

Either one of us would do. Fresh men in a small town. They're all over us."

"They don't know every embarrassing thing about us going all the way back to kindergarten. We could probably be horrible trolls and they'd still find us attractive. Not that you're a troll or anything," Kurt hastily amended. "In fact, you're less trollish now that the puppy fat is gone."

I cringed. Puppy fat? Well, I had been a little soft around the middle when I first arrived at the cabin. Blame it on a student lifestyle, where easily available pizza could overpower the gym time. I'd had a pretty good physique, only hidden under a bit of padding. At an even six feet tall, I was still a bit short for the one hundred eighty-five pounds I had been packing. Domino's didn't deliver out to the cabin, morning doughnuts were forty miles away, and I'd been doing a lot of physical labor. Three weeks away from the treats had helped me trim the middle; I'd had to take my belt in another notch this morning. The T-shirt fit tighter in the arms, too, and it wasn't because it shrank in the laundry, either. I had a good look at myself in the bathroom at the HQ. If the Lindys of the world noticed Kurt first, they still had reason to notice me.

Holy shit! Kurt had just noticed me! I swallowed hard.

He rattled away, making me hope the heat in my cheeks could be blamed on the lack of air conditioning in the crudmobile. "It can work out, though. Look at Rich and Abigail." I hadn't seen either of them since orientation: the ranger teams weren't usually in the same place at the same time unless a disaster was going on. "Abigail was working at the gas station when Rich came up from Pueblo, and they got engaged. Now they're rangers, which should be a good trial for married life."

"It's one way to get to know someone real well, I guess." I eased off the paved road and onto our dirt road, ready to rattle some more, mentally ticking off the things I'd learned about my own partner in a short amount of time, like the fact that he slept on his left side, snored when really tired, and considered the floor to be a sock's natural habitat. Then something else dawned on me. "You weren't thrilled about Lindy and Tanya coming out to fix dinner, et cetera, et cetera. Sounded like there could have been a lot of et cetera." I forced an image out of my mind of Kurt and Tanya rolling on a blanket out by the lake— but not before mentally pushing Tanya into the ice-cold water.

"I'm picky. Face it, Jake, this is a small town, and we're a nice addition to the male landscape. And Rich is kind of a cautionary tale, even though I like Abigail. We could sure get laid, but how much do you want to bet we'd end up with angry daddies marching us down to Pastor Blivens at shotgun point?"

"Is that what happened to Rich?" I hadn't heard anything like that, but I'd been mostly listening to Kurt these last few weeks. I'm sure Lindy could have filled me in, if I weren't terrified of being alone with her.

"No. I think Abigail arm-wrestled Lindy, Dawn, and Tanya for him." We broke out laughing.

Soon our homestead came into sight, but I bypassed the cabin, making a beeline for our new refrigerator. Kurt had enough fun at my expense today that I whistled a jaunty tune on the backward journey to the water, unaccompanied by the sound of pine on paintwork. Not that anyone would detect a few more scratches on my old beat-up car. Kurt glared at me sideways until we passed the evergreen that had sprouted to be his nemesis.

"Where did you want to hang the pulley?" Kurt asked as we surveyed the lakeshore for likely trees.

"See that limb? It should work there." I pointed to a sturdy cottonwood that stuck out over the water.

"Hang it there and it'll foul the Tarzan rope," Kurt warned.

"Which is more important, playing Tarzan or having cold food?" I knew which way I voted, but the rope would be a lot of fun. We hadn't used it yet—the lake hadn't warmed up enough for more than a quick bath. A dip in the swimming hole would be a whole different kind of experience since I'd started noticing him in a big way, and now that the weather was getting warmer, Kurt would probably suggest it soon. I hadn't brought swim trunks with me and didn't know if Kurt had, so that could be reeeeal interesting.

"The food, but… maybe we can hang it separately enough that we can have both." Kurt took off his heavy boots, stuck the pulley and the hank of thin rope in the leg pockets of his utilities, and started to shim up the tree. I could only watch in amazement—I thought we'd have to bring the tank truck down to stand on that. Must be that old rock-climbing background Kurt had mentioned. He got out on the limb to tie the pulley on after cutting the cord to length with his pocketknife.

"Okay, throw me the rope. I'll thread it through."

Trying to throw the end of an unweighted rope is kind of frustrating. I tossed it, but it fell way short of Kurt's waving hand; I had to reel in the wet nylon twice. The third time, I tied our new chunk of parmesan cheese to the end, and the weight made it a lot easier to throw. Like my archery, my throwing was almost accurate enough. The cheese flew within inches of his hand, close enough to tempt Kurt into lunging after it. Mistake—he overbalanced and fell headfirst out of the tree, screaming and flailing all the way down into the water.

I laughed out loud when he surfaced, spitting out a stream of lake water, hair plastered flat to his scalp. "How deep is it out there?" I called, knowing it was well past eight feet.

I got a crusty look for that on his swim back to the shore. "Deep enough," he replied.

Once on shore, he untied the cheese from the rope and threw it at me like a fastball. He peeled off the T-shirt, gone dark from the water. Wringing it out, he made a puddle at his feet as muscles rippled in his arms and chest. The shirt got draped over a fallen log to dry before he tied the end of the rope around his waist and headed back up the tree. This time I watched his bare arms and back, and dropping my eyes let me see the wet cotton clinging to his ass as he scaled the trunk. I had to look away before my body responded to that, so I started packaging food into the gallon zipper bags, pressing the air out as best I could, then sucking out the rest. That got me a funny look from Kurt, but he had the good grace not to comment. Soon he'd skittered back down onto the ground, and we rigged the box with both ends of the rope, one to raise and lower, the other to pull the box toward shore.

"First, a wet run," I decided, so we dipped the box into the water and retrieved it without incident. Putting the food in changed the balance—too many heavy things must have been on one side. The box came out of the water, draining in cascades from all the holes, then it slipped to one side and opened. All the precious food flipped into the lake.

"Shit!" we yelped. I started pulling off my boots, and Kurt peeled out of his soggy utilities. The wet clothing would be a danger as we went down to the bottom to retrieve our goodies, so I peeled down, too, more easily since my clothes were still dry. Still no underwear, since I hadn't been able to find a way to smuggle any into the bathroom at HQ. Didn't matter now. I wrapped a bight of rope around a rock to fix the box in place over the water and then followed Kurt into the lake.

We dived and surfaced, hands full, loading some of the

prizes into the dangling box, then taking things to shore when the box didn't look like it could take any more safely in its tilted position.

"Did you find the mayonnaise?" I asked, once we'd both been down and back twice, empty-handed. The water wasn't clear enough to find anything by sight, so we were hunting by touch. Electricity zinged through my body the time I'd grasped what I thought were hotdogs and came up clutching Kurt's hand.

"No, I thought you did," Kurt said as he treaded water.

"Damn, I really wanted that mayonnaise," I said. I resigned myself to another chilly trip downward. Kurt twisted in the water and did a tucked surface dive, shooting to the bottom as he uncoiled his legs, which gave me a brief look at his package before he submerged. That couldn't have been intentional, and I was grateful for the cold water that would hinder me from sprouting wood. I'd seen him naked before, but that was before. Now I was noticing, and as naked as he.

Almost oxygenated enough to go down again to help hunt, I had started to turn in the water when Kurt surfaced next to me. Actually, he'd nearly come up underneath me, and he stroked the length of my body as he rose to the air. Pushing off me to gain a little distance, he planted a foot on my thigh, dangerously close to my groin. The cold water was my ally, I reminded myself—the faceful of splashing would help me not react.

"Success!" he crowed, waving the jar around. "Is that everything?"

"I think so," I said, and we swam to shore.

"Careful," he warned as we pulled the dangling box over to land. "I don't really want to go after all that again." Me either, I thought, though if he brushed against me again, I wouldn't mind. I only wished he'd done it on purpose.

We rigged a cradle for the box, using more of the thin rope that Kurt had used to secure the pulley to the tree. Kurt hadn't put his clothes back on, which meant that I couldn't either without calling attention to my nakedness. Chilly enough to not embarrass myself, I bit the inside of my cheek when I got too much of a look at Kurt's body. He squatted to tie the cord with some complicated climber's knot that he assured me would not come undone accidentally. Then we secured the box around with the forgotten bungee cords, a move that would have saved considerable trouble had we done it half an hour earlier. Satisfied that the box wouldn't tilt now that the rope went through a few of the drain holes, no matter how badly unbalanced it was, we lowered our fridge into the water.

"That box is on belay," he said with a grin. "It goes nowhere now, unless we move it."

"All right!" We high-fived each other, and then Kurt flopped onto the grass in a sunny spot, on, dear Lord, his back. He clasped his hands together under his head after selecting a stem of grass to chew on, and raised one knee. This was nothing new —the only new thing was how much I wanted to run my hands over him.

"Want to swim some more after we warm up?" he suggested around his grass stem, which waggled in the air. "See if the fridge box and the Tarzan rope are compatible?"

"I'm pretty cold," I said, and that was only the truth. My teeth wanted to chatter, but warming up would endanger my composure. Looking at Kurt would really endanger my composure, so I shaded my eyes, pretending a great interest in a something or other across the lake. "I think I'll start dinner." That gave me the excuse to pick up my clothes and dress, pants first.

"Do you usually go commando?" which was a stupid question for him to ask; he'd seen me get dressed often enough to know. Oh shit, it meant he was looking. At least I wasn't hard.

"No, I forgot to throw any clean shorts on the pile this morning," I replied, cursing my flawed memory.

"Did you remember to save out the stuff you wanted to cook with, or did it all go into the water?" he asked.

"Damn, it's all in the box." Okay, I'd been distracted.

"Early onset Alzheimer's, it's a bitch." Kurt sat up to put his boots on. "See you up at the cabin." He stood up and then bent to grab his wet clothing, which he slung over his shoulder rather than putting it on. After all, I was the only one around to see, right?

Kurt headed up the hill, wearing nothing but boots, whistling some tune that sounded vaguely like Joan Jett's "Do You Wanna Touch Me?" Nah, couldn't be. Hauling up the box was a good reason to drag my eyes away before he turned around and caught me looking at him with the longing I was sure showed on every feature. I didn't want to watch him walk away naked—I wanted to watch him walk toward me naked. Rummaging in the box let me catch glimpses before he disappeared around the curve, the dark green fabric covering only his shoulder and back. My body remembered how he'd slipped against me as he rose from the bottom of the lake, mayonnaise in hand.

He'd been so close, and still so far.

FOURTEEN

Breakfast was delicious. Kurt cooked, and a good thing too; I would probably have burnt everything from sleepy inattention. Last night had been horrible. I'd forced myself not to toss and turn, but sleep didn't come for a long time. I could hear Kurt's soft breathing from less than ten feet away, but it might as well have been miles for all I could go to him.

The memory of him walking up the hill in nothing but his boots would have killed sleep all by itself. Wet, green clothing tossed over his shoulder slapped against his bare skin, and I'd only been able to sneak peeks while I fished things back out of the box. Thinking about that around midnight sent me out of the cabin to relieve tension, when I ducked into the trees and let myself remember his broad shoulders tapering to his waist and the way the muscles in his ass flexed as he ambled off. The red fox that made his rounds by our cabin lolled his tongue in the moonlight at me when I was done. I threw a pine cone at him for catching me at it.

I didn't know how much more of this I could take. He could be upset at the way I burned for him, or he might think I was a pervert for wanting him. He might give me the sideways beady eye for the rest of the season, never being at ease with me again, or he could tell me to get the hell out. Or worse, he might make a mad dash to HQ, demanding reassignment immediately, though the Chief hadn't agreed to that before. My blood ran cold at the thought of being outed, especially in a small town where rumors traveled like wildfire. I imagined Lindy and Dawn, rocks in hand, hiding Kurt behind their backs.

Maybe getting out of the Forest Service would be the better answer. Running seemed like the right thing to do around 2:00 a.m. Then Kurt would never have to know how much I wanted him, he'd never have the chance to tell me no. He'd never have a reason to think less of me for what I wanted to do with him. Why, oh why had I thought a summer spent rangering a good idea? *I'll get away*, I'd told myself, *figure out what I want to do with my life*. Weigh that whole "am I or ain't I" question. After four years of close quarters with roommates who never clued in, keeping my secret in the wild of the Colorado Rockies should be a piece of cake, right? Well, at least it decisively answered the question. I definitely, beyond the shadow of any doubt, wanted a man. And not any old man, but one in particular: Kurt Carlson.

He'd have other reasons to think less of me, though. At 2:10 I remembered that he'd been happy earlier, when I said I wasn't leaving the Forest Service. So running would disappoint him, especially if my reasons sounded like cowardice about fire. I wondered if I could pull off a lie about family responsibilities.

A newly awakened Kurt lifted an eyebrow but said nothing at my worn appearance—the shaving mirror confirmed that the sleeplessness had marked me. He might have had some inkling of the thoughts going through my mind, because he didn't take the opportunity to twit me as he usually would. Maybe it was all going to come crumbling down on me anyway. The blue sky had that kind of omen in it—a front showed as a wall of gray-white cumulonimbus clouds to the northwest. Rain would be a good thing for this parched land but there was no guarantee we'd get it.

The morning patrol proved uneventful. A good thing, because I missed most of it. The rumble of the big diesel engine lulled me to sleep more than it kept me awake. After the third head bob, Kurt tossed me a jacket and told me to curl up and sleep for a while. "I'll wake you if anything happens. You aren't going to be one damned bit of good like that. You might as well catch a couple of Zs."

My dreams were jumbled and strange; this wasn't going to be really restful sleep. Kurt kept talking to me in these dreams, telling me all the things I wanted to hear, when I could under-stand the words. Trees and motorbikes dueled weirdly as I shot at formless things with the bow and missed.

I must have drifted into a better sleep after a while, because the dreams stopped, and I became vaguely aware of being more comfortable. A pillow beneath my cheek helped, and then I was out like the proverbial light. No dreams, no thoughts.

The peace shattered some unknown time later, but I sure didn't wake on my own. Kurt shook my shoulder, saying, "Jake, wake up! Come on, wake up!"

"Wha...?" became "Ow!" when my face connected sharply with the steering wheel. Flopping back where I'd started plopped my head on Kurt's thigh, and I grabbed my battered nose with both hands. My eyes scrunched shut from the blow and stars danced behind my closed eyelids. I could barely register where I was or what had happened.

"Guess you're awake now," Kurt observed wryly as I sat up, more cautiously this time. "Anything broken?"

"Don't think so." I smoothed my fingers over my nose gingerly.

"Good, because we have a fire to put out."

FIFTEEN

Kurt got from first gear to third in a hurry, bringing us closer to the visible smoke point. He found, or made, a spot wide enough to get the truck off the road—I said nothing about the last time Kurt had scraped the tanker's sides on vegetation.

The Chief took down our coordinates over the radio during the short trip, promised to send someone else over if we needed it, and warned us that erratic winds were being reported all over the National Forest. "There's a storm moving in, but it might be dry, boys." We groaned at that because dry storms carried lightning and one fire was enough.

We jumped out of the truck to extract the things we needed: our heavy, fire-retardant pants and jackets, helmets, air tanks, shovels, and axes. I eyed the fire shelters in their vinyl bags. "Think we should take these?"

"No, I don't think it's that big of a fire. We should have it out pretty fast." Kurt slung the axe over his shoulder.

A small amount of smoke curled up out of the trees. The whine of an engine made me pull my head out of the equipment locker on the side of the truck in time to see the red

RAV4 come careening around the bend. They didn't stop—they actually sped up going past us, hauling out of range without stopping.

Sweat started to trickle down my back even with the jacket open as we marched into the trees, going farther, once again, than we could squirt with the hose. A cigarette butt trail led us straight to the fire site. Max's lesson in manners hadn't stuck. What we found looked not much worse than what we'd coped with the other day, though this time human stupidity caused the fire. Asshats, burning my woods.

The smoking litter led from the road to what had been a camp site. The tent itself had been reduced to a few charred shreds of fabric on poles that curved into the air in the center of a circle of burning pine duff. The trees grew thick here, tall and thin, fighting to reach the light with their green upper branches. Lower branches had lost the race to the sun, forfeited their needles to become dry snags. Everything around the tent amounted to dry fuel—bad conditions for a fire to get loose.

"I think if we clear a fire break over here, we can keep it from getting into the trees," Kurt said, and we started scraping the earth clean. Starving the fire would work better than trying to put it out directly—I'd learned that much from last week's efforts. We worked diligently and were nearly two thirds around the fire zone when the wind whipped up.

"Shit!" Kurt sprinted for a section of the fire zone that started expanding a whole lot faster as the wind pushed the flames. I followed, knowing that he wanted to keep the ground fire from hitting the trees, and we scraped frantically around two of the endangered pines, but the third caught fire before we could get there.

Flame licked up the trunk and tasted the branches. "It's

candling," Kurt snarled, craning his head to peer into the treetops.

The fire was consuming the tree from the base up and had already spread along the lower limbs. I craned upward, too, looking for what else would be in danger from this tree.

"The one damned beetle-killed pine on this acre and it's right there!" He whipped the axe around. "If we take it down, away from the candle, it won't take the fire into the crown." He started chopping, and I cleared ground around the candling tree lest the fire spread further. The wind continued whipping around, blowing smoke into our faces and making sparks jump into the air. I coughed violently to clear a lungful of smoke, the heat and ash stinging my eyes. The fickle wind seemed to change direction every few seconds, which raised the risks—we couldn't be in every place at once.

"Push from here!" Kurt had his hands on the partly severed trunk, so I helped him shove the tree over, away from the fire. Satisfied that the most dangerous bit of ladder fuel wasn't going to burn now, we considered what to do next. The wind howled, pelting us with debris; once again it had shifted directions. Now it pushed the fire back over onto ground that had already burned, or that had fire break scraped, which made the wind our ally.

That didn't last. The air currents changed yet again, lifting flaming bits into the air. Some went out like fireflies, others fell back onto burned ground, and a few sailed over the firebreak to land in fresh fuel. I suddenly hated the springy pine duff: it blazed too easily. We stamped out the spot fires that started, but the candling tree had not exhausted itself and now it came apart.

Fiery chunks flew in the wild wind, bouncing on the ground, shedding sparks. Some flew upward as one evil gust caught them, flipping at least one into a mostly dead tree that hadn't fallen completely. It smoldered twenty feet above our heads.

"If we take down that one?" I pointed at one tree, but Kurt swung his axe at the next one over, to bring the dead lodgepole pine down and within our reach. I started hacking at the tall pine Kurt thought supported the dead tree the most. If we tipped it right, the whole burning mess would come down onto scorched ground to die.

Too late. The dead tree became its own funeral pyre as it burst into flame, crackling and popping. The wind toyed with the flames, sharing them with other trees, and it no longer mattered that two burning pines dropped onto the charred tatters of the tent.

"The operation was a success, but the patient died," Kurt quipped. We counted how many trees still standing had flames dancing in their tops. "It is now officially bigger than the two of us. Let's get out of here."

"What if we took out the trees at the perimeter?" I asked, but I gathered my equipment anyway.

"Won't help. The perimeter is too big because the wind keeps changing. We can chop away while it blows fire over there." Kurt pointed at a tree on the far side of the burnt circle that had orange licks curling around the trunk. "Come on!" He set off at a brisk pace back to the truck. "We need a look at the map."

Remembering glumly that wind could carry fire long distances, knowing that a crown fire was well beyond the ability of two men to extinguish, I followed Kurt back to the truck. But damned if my heart didn't bleed for those poor trees, and my anger blazed hotter than the pines for the girl and her stupid cigarettes.

"Think we can hit it with the water now?" I asked. I slung my shovel onto its hook and slammed the cargo door.

"Not going to stick around to find out," Kurt told me. "The wind is so crazy that the fire is spreading fast. Count trees." He got into the driver's seat and picked up the microphone.

I counted flaming pines with a knife digging into my guts to see that the number had nearly doubled while we hiked back. Kurt shouted into the radio at the Chief. I tuned back in to what they were saying when the Chief's voice crackled out, "Head out to a safe distance. We may have to let this one burn out against the scarp. Got a dozer team headed to the east of you now."

"Roger that. Out," Kurt finished. The wind whipped fire into another two trees.

"Don't we have enough distance now?" I asked. "The trees are about fifty yards off the road. There's just this scrubby stuff here."

"This scrubby stuff is gambel oak." Kurt turned over the diesel engine. The noise made me pause, so before I could ask a stupid question I remembered that I knew the significance of gambel oak.

"Gotcha," I said, still counting, but the flames went back too far to see. "How fast do you think this fire is expanding?

Kurt did some calculations in his head. "It's not going to set any records," he said, throwing the big diesel into gear, "but if it was moving fourteen miles a day, it would have gotten us already and it would take out Rendezvous Lake Lodge before tomorrow night. The dozer team is between them and the fire. They should be fine. Us, on the other hand...."

Oh shit. I didn't like that sound of that. Just because it wasn't moving at Storm King speeds didn't mean the fire wasn't expanding really fast. "What's our problem?"

"Jake, did you or did you not learn to read a map?" Kurt fought the steering wheel to the sharpest turn possible, smashing into gambel oaks front and back. In other words, by his usual Braille system, though to be fair, it was a one-lane road with tall bushes on either side. Given what that brush would do once alight, I didn't begrudge a few scratches and a bit of testiness.

So I grabbed the map, a USGS topological map, and looked at it. "Where do I start looking?" I stared stupidly at the map—falling asleep had left me uncertain where we were.

The truck pointed the other way at last, so he took a moment to stab a finger to the page. "Here."

It took me a minute to figure out the problem. "This road ends about a mile up, so we're turning around instead of getting caught on a dead end. Whoa, I bet the RAV4 people went up and found out they'd trapped themselves."

"Yeah. If they even had a map. So, we'll go back the other way instead of sticking around with all these nice green incendiaries." Kurt glanced at the huge clouds of smoke billowing from the forest, and his foot got heavier on the accelerator. "We want to get at least seven miles away. Look at the map and tell me why that is."

"Because that puts us seven miles away from the fire?" Looking at the wavy lines on the topo map wasn't telling me enough, apparently, because he snorted.

"We can't go the other way, at least not and stay with the truck, and we need to get past where the scarp ends." I was going to have to ask another probably dumb question, but he decided to give me *Map Reading for the Compleat Ignoramus*, chapter four. "See all those lines really close together? That means steep terrain. Now look to our left and tell me how those things go together."

It would help if I knew what the hell a scarp was, but I could see gambel oak stretching maybe a half mile to a rather imposing cliff that ran back behind us a long way and stretched out parallel to the road a long way ahead. The map showed the wavy lines separating about six miles ahead, so the cliff must be the scarp. "Because if we don't, we risk getting trapped between something we can't climb and the fire."

"Right, and...." Before he could finish the thought, the wind had changed yet again, blowing massive amounts of smoke and dirt across the road. Visibility went to nothing, so Kurt slackened speed, but not soon enough to let him avoid an obstacle that he would rather have gone around. We'd known this thing was there, we'd avoided it the other day, I realized, but we took that damned rock in the road at about twenty-five miles an hour with one wheel.

The impact was enough to swing the medium-duty truck halfway around, so the rear wheels caught in the brush. Two tons of water in the back kept right on going, though. We tipped up on one set of wheels, giving us a sickening moment of vertigo at the top. For six horrible heartbeats I thought we were going to go right on over, but the backsplash in the tank knocked us back onto six tires. We were sitting with a distinct list, but we were upright.

Not that it did us much good. Kurt and I both scrambled out of the truck to assess the damage.

"Damn it!" Kurt and I swore with dismay over the blown front tire. We chucked our heavy fire jackets to one side, preparing to deal with this latest setback. I slung myself under the truck to grab the jack.

With one eye each toward the blazing trees, we shoved that jack into position and took turns pumping the handle to raise the truck high enough to get the weight off the split tire and then farther to get the axle high enough to put the spare on. Sweat pooled under my arms and on my breastbone. Kurt's shirt grew dark and stuck to his back with the exertion of yanking the handle up and down.

"It would have to be a front tire," I grumbled as I wrestled the sixty-five pound spare out from under the chassis. If it had been a rear tire, we could limp along on the redundancy of the other two tires on that side, but with damage to the front, we had to take time for repairs. I rolled the spare along the ground to where Kurt was wrenching the tire iron around and around to remove the bolts on the damaged tire. On the fourth bolt, Kurt leaned his full weight on the tire iron, but it didn't budge until I leaned on it with him. Horrible screeching sounded like the bolt stripping, but it turned at last. The fifth bolt didn't fight us, giving me time to throw the casualty to one side into the brush. If the tire survived the flames, we'd salvage it later, and if it didn't, we'd count the cost cheap, but time wasn't our friend now. The wind pushed smoke and ash into our skins. I coughed, ash and pine sap heavy on my tongue. The last wood smoke I'd tasted had been in Max's luscious barbeque, which had only threatened to kill me for gluttony.

Kurt and I heaved the spare tire, struggling with the weight as we mated the holes in the rim with the bolts. What would have been a moderate task if we were fresh was burdensome now while we were tired from fighting the fire and growing more frantic by the minute. The encroaching flames growled like some monstrous beast. I fumbled the nuts onto the bolts, dropping one into the dirt, where it rolled under the truck. I swore and tried to dive after it.

"Leave it, Jake. We'll be okay," Kurt said with one hand gripping my arm. "Four bolts will get us out of here." He turned the iron again, tightening the nuts into drivability.

After we finished the exchange, Kurt looked at me wryly. "It never rains but it pours," his face seemed to say, but we said nothing. We just scrambled into the cab. The flames had advanced toward us, a thumb of fire reaching out into the gambel oaks, trying to find the road. I'd always liked the scent of burning oak, but this was no fireplace. The smell wouldn't mean home any more, only danger after this.

"Let's get out of here," Kurt suggested. He turned the key to bring the big diesel to life. "It's going to get hot."

"No shit." I looked out at the fire coming toward us. "Can we go, already?"

"Okay." Kurt threw the truck into gear and stepped on the pedal. We didn't move, though the truck howled. He tried wrenching the gearshift into what should have been first gear, which didn't look like a different position than before, let out the clutch, and stepped on the accelerator again. We didn't move. A ghastly grinding rumbled up from below and behind the cab. "What the fuck?"

He tried reverse, but nothing happened except that the noise changed from a grinding scream to a metallic clank.

"Kurt, stop! You'll take out the transmission if you keep that up!" I deciphered what had happened: something essential broke when the truck smashed back onto the level. "The pinion gear is gone! That's a couple days in the shop, at least."

"Fuck!" Kurt smashed his hand against the steering wheel.

"What do we do now?" I yelled back, more out of frustration than hope that he'd know. The fire here extended well past the edge of the pine forest. The wind was shifting crazily again and would blow the flames beyond the road soon. The edge of the conflagration was too low to see, but explosions announced burning gambel oak becoming superheated. I wanted to be well away from brush that turned to flaming shrapnel.

"Start walking, Jake."

Kurt tossed down the map and picked up the radio. "Bad news, Chief. The truck is cratered. We hit a rock and busted the pinion gear. It's not going anywhere." For a moment we got no response, and then the Chief's voice crackled out.

"I'll send Rich and Abigail after you. Stay put. ETA in one point seven five hours."

"No can do, Chief. Fire's coming this way." The wind had changed again, bringing the stink of smoke through the vents. "We're going to head out. I think we can get around the fire and up Road Twelve far enough to be out of range. But yeah, send...."

I missed the rest of the conversation because I got out of the truck, armed with an idea. The pump gurgled on, the hose filled, and I started squirting five hundred gallons of water at the brush around the truck.

"What the fuck are you doing?" Kurt screamed into the wind. He'd finished talking with the Chief and followed me out of the truck.

"I'm laying a wet line!" I screeched back. "It might help."

"Getting our asses out of here would really help!" he yelled, this time out of anger rather than trying to be heard over the wind, which had hit an inexplicable lull.

"Yeah, well, the fire isn't advancing right now, so it doesn't matter! It might save the truck if it does come this way." I kept spraying water in a large semicircle around the truck. It would be great to salvage the truck, but it would be even better not to see if exploding gambel oak or exploding diesel fuel created more havoc.

"It would be more time for us to haul ass!" Kurt insisted. "Come on!"

"I have another hundred fifty gallons to lay down. Go get

stuff while I do it." Might as well empty the tank: that water sure wasn't doing any good where it was.

"It's going to evaporate before the fire gets here," he warned but went to get more water and the fire shelters out of compartments in the sides of the truck.

The pump coughed dry, so I left the hose on the ground. I wasn't going to demand the time to coil it. The wind huffed insistently again, but parallel to the flames now, and I hoped it would stay that way since it was blowing the eastern edge of the fire back on itself. I didn't think there would be a western edge because we'd put that side out pretty much. If we were lucky it would put itself out that way on the eastern side, but we couldn't depend on it. I shrugged back into my protective jacket and went to collect my share of the equipment. Kurt had laid out the fire shelters, extra oxygen tanks, and all the spare drinking water bottles we had. With luck, the two gallons would be enough. Without, they'd be enough for the rest of our lives.

"Saddle up, Jake." Kurt heaved his folded shelter, which was a bit bigger than a scuba tank, onto his back and collected some more air tanks. I filled my pockets with water bottles, hoisted my own gear, and we set off down the road. We marched silently, sometimes because the wind veered on us and we needed the masks, sometimes because there just didn't seem to be anything to say.

SIXTEEN

Tired before we ever abandoned the truck, we could be out of range in two or two and a half hours, I judged, at the pace we were able to make. I tried not to think about anything more than putting one foot in front of the other, and I looked at nothing more than the road. Someone might be by to get us before we'd gotten past the scarp, but only if we stayed on the road instead of going cross country on a shortcut.

A bad gust of wind blew into us, slowing our pace, making every step twice the effort. When it changed, it buffeted us from the side, not exactly an improvement because now it brought more ash and smoke, obscuring the roadbed. Kurt and I could see each other enough not to collide, and that was about it. Too bad the elk outran their visibility.

The herd, which might have numbered only six or seven but felt like ten thousand, came bounding out of the smoke at us, spooked by the fire. Big animals seemed bigger for coming out of nowhere, their brown backs as high as my chest. Wide, tall, and frightened, they knocked us back and forth as they passed us, throwing us against their herdmates. We were helpless in the short maelstrom, bouncing from one hairy assailant to another, ending in the dusty roadbed. The herd disappeared as quickly as it came.

"Fuck!" My heart tried to leap from my chest and follow the elk. I rolled off lumps of equipment. I was only bruised, but —"Kurt! Are you all right?" He wasn't moving.

"I am going—" He paused and grunted. "—to come back during hunting season and shoot every last one of those damned elk." He sat up in stages, elbows to hands to upright, and reached to his ankle. He probed inside his boot, hissing. "I don't know if I twisted it or if one of those damned things stepped on me, but my ankle is shot."

"You probably twisted it, because you'd be bleeding if they stepped on you." I'd dropped my fire shelter during the stampede, and now it had huge rips—there was no point even picking it up again except to toss it out of the road. I put my mask on to look upwind to the fire, trying to judge where the leading edge was relative to us. The answer wasn't good. "Can you walk?"

He flexed the ankle and got next to no motion out of it before he hissed in pain again. "I'm going to have to. Help me up."

What might have been a really bad idea in better circumstances was necessary now, but the damage would be compounded by putting weight on it, I thought. "We need another idea, Kurt. The fire is running parallel to us and coming this way. You aren't going to outrun it on that leg." I yanked him to his feet. "What's over that way?"

He touched his toe to the ground and tried to stand. "The scarp. We can run away faster that way, but our ride won't find us."

"Our ride will find two crispy rangers if we keep to the road."

Kurt dragged the map out of his pocket and sank back to sitting. He ripped the map open. "I think if we head up to the scarp, there's a place we can hole up until morning. Max and I found it last fall when we were bringing my elk out." He ran his finger over the close wavy lines, looking for some feature only he would recognize.

Since I was coughing and my eyes were streaming, I was ready to believe him. "What is this place?" I'd have put my mask back on, but then we couldn't talk.

"Cave." He kept hunting. "Jake, I think we've only come about a quarter mile from the truck. We're going to have to let the Chief know plans have changed."

I didn't want to leave him; I couldn't bear it if he wasn't okay when I returned—if nothing else lunged from the smoke to prevent me from returning. "I can get there and back pretty fast, Kurt." I shed all the equipment except my fire suit. "Keep an eye on this, okay? And use the shelter if it looks like you need to." I couldn't look back again to where he sat in the road after I rested my hand on his shoulder. Dear Lord, I hoped he wouldn't need to. *Please, dear Lord, please keep him safe.*

Scouts' pace, a hundred paces jogging, a hundred paces walking, would get me to the truck and back fast enough, but without overwhelming me in my exhausted state. Running was tempting but probably beyond me now—I couldn't jeopardize completing the trip. Nothing, not even my own body, could prevent me from returning to Kurt. Counting my paces used most of my remaining brain—I nearly ran into the truck before I realized it was there. I got on the radio as soon as my breath came back enough to speak.

"Chief, Jake here. Change of plans. Cancel the ride."

He crackled back at me, "What happened?"

"We got run over by a herd of elk about a quarter mile from the truck. Kurt's injured, and he's waiting for me to get back." The stretcher mocked me from the back of the truck, completely useless without a third person, as the boy had observed a few days or an eternity ago.

"How bad?"

"His ankle's injured, but I can move him. Staying on the road isn't safe—the fire's advancing too fast—but we're headed to the scarp. Kurt says there's a cave."

"Where exactly?"

"Don't know the coordinates. Truck's here." I rattled off the coordinates from the truck's GPS. "It's somewhere up the scarp. Kurt thinks he can find it again, and Max from Rendezvous Lake Lodge knows it from elk hunting. If we have to, we'll stay on the scarp. It's rock." I didn't have time to argue with him. "Chief, I have to go get Kurt before the fire does. Ask Max. We'll be there." I dropped the radio and collected the bigger first aid kit because the small one in my pocket didn't have anything Kurt needed in there.

The distance back to Kurt seemed at least twice as long as from Kurt to the truck. I glanced fearfully at the fire as I trotted back to him, when the wind permitted it. If he'd been overrun, or thought he'd be overrun, he'd get into the shelter; he could get it open and zipped around him even with his injury. I kept reminding myself that neither his hands nor his brain had been damaged. He'd survive where he was, but could I get back to him?

Yes. I could. The wind had changed again, and I could see Kurt sitting there in his mask, looking toward the flames with one hand on his shelter. I yelled to him, hoping he could hear through the roar of the fire, but he didn't turn his head until I was nearly upon him. Grateful that we had nothing to fold back up, we could load and head away from the flames.

"Hey, buddy. Let's get out of here!" I offered a hand, which he took to swing to one foot. Reloading my pockets and shouldering the remaining shelter took a few minutes. Kurt started to argue with me but stopped, deciding I could handle the equipment better that way. "Where to?"

Hooking his arm around my neck let me put my arm around his back to catch him beneath his opposite arm. I'd be his other leg, because he wasn't touching the damaged foot to the ground.

"Straight out into the oak, Jake. I think I'll know where after we get some distance. We may need to turn east a ways." He said nothing about how long my trip back to the truck had taken, nor about being left all alone; he only lifted his chin with fortitude and we set off into the brush.

The oaks were patchy, with enough room to travel between them two abreast in most places, though they caught at our clothing. A few green-lobed leaves swatted as high as our faces, but the oaks were mostly short enough to see over, thanks to the grazing of the thousands of elk that lived in the national forest. They were taller closer to town, where the animals didn't come, but here they didn't obscure the scarp. We drew nearer with excruciating slowness.

Kurt leaned on me heavily when he tried putting his injured foot down, but still he limped badly. I would not let him try this unassisted, game though he was. Instead, I dragged him sideways between the crooked branches, which bent to our passing, and even through places where the oaks grew close enough to interlace and it was too far to go around. Once, I stopped and insisted he drink some of the water, then tried to put the bottle back in my jacket pocket without him noticing.

"Drink," he ordered me. "I'm hurt, I'm not ill or stupid, and you're more dehydrated than me." Busted, I drank, wondering why I'd thought he wouldn't notice.

"Veer toward the left," he told me when he found his bearings. "Line up with that tall tree and the lopsided boulder. Not far now."

I followed Kurt's directions, trusting that he could find the place again before the monster chasing us caught up. I tried not to look at the fire too often because it reached well into the gambel oak now. Echoes of explosions boomed off the scarp. Hope burned along with the brush—I hoped Kurt's cave would be enough to get us through the fire.

"Almost there, Jake. See it?" Kurt steered us to the left before we reached the rock wall.

"No—oh." A dark smudge when seen from a distance, the cave mouth became an opening up close. He hadn't mentioned it being seven feet off the ground. I had nasty visions of barbecue grills above the coals. The vista would be spectacular —I just hoped we didn't get a steak's-eye view.

Kurt threw off his equipment. "Give me a leg up, Jake." He stuck the knee on his bad side into my cupped hands and scrambled up the wall with his good leg, ending on his belly on the ledge. I passed the shelter up first, thinking that if it came to it, we could unfurl it inside the cave while the blaze licked along the edge of the rock wall. In my mind, steaks turned to baked potatoes in foil jackets. Air tanks and water bottles went up, then he stuck his head back out. "Come on."

The edge was only a foot above my head, so I grabbed and climbed. I hadn't quite gotten my upper body over the ledge when my footing crumbled. I started to slide out, but Kurt grabbed my arm and hauled. He was kneeling, so his giant yank pulled me almost onto him. I landed nearly across his knees, something I would have appreciated more in other circumstances, especially since he gasped with pain from me jostling his injury. I rolled to a sitting position before turning to see where he'd brought us.

"All the comforts of home," he said wryly. We shed the heavy fire suits, turning them inside out to dry before dropping them on the floor of the cave. We'd marched with the jackets open, but we'd still sweated through our T-shirts. My thirst and tiredness could be measured by how much I wanted to look at the water bottle instead of him. We drank, torn between conserving our supplies for what could be a stay of days and the need to replenish all the water making our shirts stick to our torsos. Evaporation started right off and felt damned good.

"Time to look at the leg, Kurt." I brought the big first aid kit over to where he sat leaning against the cave wall and unlacing his boot. "Let me do that." I spread the laces widely before easing the boot away from his ankle, trying not to bend it. His lips thinned before I had the sock off, exposing the puffy ankle. I'd dreamed of undressing him, but not like this.

"No hoof marks," I noted. "You must have twisted it on the way down."

"Probably," he agreed, eyes closed. "This ankle always seems to be the one to get it. I brace it to ski."

The kit contained an ACE bandage which I used to strap him. "We'll have to RICE you as best we can. Rest: well, after our little journey, you're going to have to rest. Compression: here we are." I secured the ends of the wrap with the clips. "Elevation: here, lift." I stuck the fire shelter under his calf, which raised it about eight inches.

"Ice would feel good," he noted, naming the missing letter of the acronym, the closest to a complaint that he'd made all day.

"Knew I forgot something," I jested weakly as I poured a bit of precious water on the ACE wrap, hoping evaporation would cool the joint. The kit also contained ibuprofen; he swallowed three tablets with a sip of water. I couldn't do much else for him with the meager supplies we had, but we'd covered the essentials.

"How far back does this go?" I asked, after a short breather where all I could do was lean against the wall.

"Not sure," he said. Kurt sat with one knee up and his head tipped back, the picture of exhaustion. We'd shoveled, chopped, toted, wrenched, and run for our lives: he earned the weariness. When he opened his eyes again, their blue was startling in the smudges marring his face, and I supposed that I had smoke and dirt all over me too. Rubbing a sleeve over my face probably rearranged the mess.

"No bears, though," I tried to joke, though a cranky, giant carnivore lunging out of the dark was about all we needed to complete the day. Blinking into the cave to adjust my eyes let me see, eventually, that a rocky, uneven floor sloped up to meet the ceiling about ten feet in. No bears, just a big rock pretending to be a bear. Once my heart quit pounding, I draped over it belly first, letting the stone pull the heat out of my body.

Someone's stomach rumbled, might have been mine. Lunch, what lunch? We'd been chopping down trees. No point in complaining.

"Here." Kurt stirred enough to dig something out of an inside pocket of his fire jacket. "Must be my night to cook."

Smashed sandwiches never tasted so good. Pickles and potato chip crumbs washed down with warm water were five-star fare tonight, though we sure could have done without what passed for candlelight outside. The wind had shifted any number of times as we hiked here, and now it blew toward the scarp again, sending smoke in with us. The bear rock became our windbreak, which Kurt traveled behind on his hands, one foot, and butt, only letting me help by moving the shelter to keep his foot up. He had vetoed using the masks yet, since our need might become a lot greater before the danger passed. I don't know how he managed to fall asleep leaning against that rock.

Wired and exhausted is a bad combination, worse when it's coupled with fear. I sat next to my partner, listening to his breathing the way I'd listened so often in the night. Then, it had meant all was right with the world, but now it was the only right thing happening. I couldn't sleep, I wouldn't wake him, so I sat alone with my thoughts, mostly ugly. It had all gone so bad, so fast. Kurt had been my biggest issue until the wind whipped up, bringing us real trouble. Now looking at him was the only good thing in my world.

Asleep, he looked so vulnerable that it was all I could do not to touch him. His head tipped back against the rock—exhaustion had to have overwhelmed him, or he would have made a nest on the cave floor. My own nap in the truck this morning came back to me with a shock. Had he looked at me and seen something similar? Could he possibly have wanted to touch me?

My nose stung with the smoke and throbbed with the injury I'd done it when he woke me. I smacked it on the steering wheel, and the only way I could have done that was if my head had been in his lap. Memory replayed my troubled sleep growing comfortable with a pillow; he moved me, or he didn't object when I fell, and his hand had been resting on my side. I'd felt safe enough to sleep deeply.

Kurt's head lolled alarmingly, and he made no effort to recover. Safety wasn't something I could offer him—we were as safe as we were going to get—but I could offer him comfort.

Gently, I lowered him down to his side and rested his head on my thigh. A deep breath and exhalation were his only response; he slept on. Napping near the fire line was a Watch Out situation for rangers, especially with unburned fuel between us and the fire, but the Standard Firefighting Orders covered this: I posted myself as his lookout.

SEVENTEEN

Kurt slept for perhaps an hour, and I might have dropped off, too, had he not stirred. When he moved, I took my hand away from his arm and then had to find an innocuous place to park it in my lap. A giant yawn creaked him once he sat up, so he may not have noticed, and he said nothing other than, "I needed that." He drew up his legs to sit cross-legged, but thought better of it and left the damaged leg outstretched. He leaned forward to rest his forehead on one bent knee to finish waking up. I could have rubbed his back from where I sat, to ease his transition to awareness, but did not.

"Anything different happen while I was out?" he asked, rubbing his eyes.

I'd been his pillow, and we were in the lee of the rock, so I'd seen nothing. "I'll check."

The wind shifted yet again, letting the air clear and allowing me to stand at the edge of the cave to assess the situation. So far, the truck seemed okay; the oaks around it hadn't burned. That might have been due more to luck than my wet line, since the fire burned patchily. Part of the land lay nearly untouched while a hundred feet to one side was scorched to black, and patches of gray-green gambel oak stood unscathed in the sea of fire. The pines still burned fiercely with a roaring that was not the wind, which shifted erratically. The light started to leave the sky, but the red and orange in the woods pretty much made up for it.

My heart sank. For now we appeared safe and sound, but Hell waited right outside our door and might come knocking before sunrise. While I might be a novice, it didn't take a seasoned firefighter to recognize that we were pretty much screwed without a miracle. "What do you suppose they'll call this fire when it's over?" I asked, swallowing back a mouthful of bile. "And do you think we'll get a nice monument?"

Kurt heaved himself to his feet and hobbled over to stand next to me. I read in the tension of his shoulders and the firm set of his jaw that he saw the same bleak fate I did. Only, once more he put on an act. I should have known the rock that was Kurt Carlson wouldn't yield without a fight. "We may or may not be toast," he murmured, taking in the boundaries of the fire as I had. "What did we do right?"

I thought hard for a moment, recalling my training and the hours he spent grilling me. "We had an escape route, even though we, uh, couldn't get all the way out with it." I couldn't blame him for the truck; I'd probably have hit the rock, too. "And we had another escape route. We knew the weather forecasts, even though the wind got us." I tried to think of what else we'd done right. "You could consider us to be posted lookouts. And it's fairly flat here to the fire, so we didn't really run uphill." The Storm King casualties had tried to escape by running uphill, though they'd had a solid wall of flame coming at them and there wasn't much choice. We'd both heard the talks. "And it isn't really downhill. Burning stuff can't roll at us. We've got the shelter." If two of us could fit. I spared a silent curse for the errant elk herd.

"Where did we screw up?" Kurt asked, and it wasn't rhetorical.

That question required no thought at all. I asked myself that same question over and over while Kurt slept. "We didn't allow enough for the wind. And we should have yelled for backup when the spot fires started."

"Maybe earlier, because of the wind."

Thinking back over the last few hours, I stood by our decisions. I'd do the same thing all over again. "It looked small and containable, Kurt."

"Yeah, but it wasn't. And we're out of contact with our supervisor now."

"A problem, but he knows where we are and what we're doing." I could tell where this was going, and yup, that's where it went.

"I should have known better, Jake. But I thought we could do it, and I may have gotten you killed." He stared down at the pebbles littering the cave floor.

"Don't take that all on yourself, Kurt." I put an arm around his shoulder, but kept my eyes on the fire. "The fire was what it was, and I didn't say anything either. I could have called for backup. I know how to use the radio. And we'd be long gone by now if it wasn't for the rock. I could have hit it as easily as you. You just happened to be driving." I squeezed him and let go, though I could have stayed like that a long time.

He didn't move away from me. "I feel responsible, though."

I knew he would. "Shut up, Kurt. You aren't." I should have kept my big mouth shut.

We were silent a long time after that, moving around only to get a drink of water. The sun set before anyone spoke again.

"If the weather wasn't so screwy, the fire would settle down once dark came." Kurt knuckled his eyes. "But with the wind, I don't know that it will."

The gambel oaks let off booms now and then, sending flaming debris flying, sometimes into unburned territory. The fire line had gotten to the other side of the road. Death crawled toward us in shades of orange and red.

I stared out the mouth of the cave at the fire while Kurt sat on his fire suit to buffer his butt from the rocks. "Wish we had a way to leave a message for the folks." Kurt had never really mentioned his family much. "They'd take this pretty hard anyway, but…."

"Yeah." I thought about my mom and dad back in Michigan, my older sister, Gramps. I was my family's fair-haired boy, and they expected great things from me, like completing my Pharm.D. and practicing my profession. They probably hoped for a few other things, too, like me marrying some sweet young woman and providing grandchildren. I'd disappointed them already by skipping my graduation ceremony to join the rangers. Getting me back in a box would devastate them, even if it permanently delayed the discussion about why the pretty bride and offspring weren't happening. I couldn't bear to think of that now. "What's your family like?" I asked for a distraction.

"My dad raised me, pretty much, after I was ten, though Larry and Vanessa helped a lot. My brother and sister, they're a lot older than me. And then when they got married—" Kurt snorted at some memory. "—Cliff and Polly got in on the act. Just what a teenage boy needs: five parent equivalents to dodge instead of the usual two. But they were good to me." He played idly with a handful of rocks. I tried to imagine two older versions of Kurt, steadfast, handsome, good at anything they set their minds to. Had they been the ones to teach Kurt how to hunt? Had the older sister taught him to cook?

"What about your mom?" Even with all that family, it sounded like a big gap in there.

"She died." Just a flat, bald statement, and Kurt put the rocks down. "She died," he whispered, and he had to be wondering if he'd be joining her soon. He didn't say anything more for a long time.

I didn't know what to do for his pain, or for my own. Whispering "I'm sorry" wasn't nearly enough, so I stayed at the mouth of the cave until the wind drove me back in. When it changed again, I resumed my lookout.

"So, is it going to get us?" Kurt finally asked, showing me a chink in his armor that I never knew existed. It made him more approachable somehow, more human. And I wanted him all the more. He'd pulled out of his memories and started watching me.

I turned to come back into the cave before the damned wind hit me with another faceful of smoke. I saw no need to lie. A seasoned firefighter like Kurt knew the score. "Maybe. This isn't the way I expected to go." Actually, I'd successfully managed to never think about dying, not personally anyway.

"Really? How did you expect to go?" Kurt watched me.

"I don't know, maybe from extreme old age, or shark bites, or something else that isn't this. Kurt, I'm twenty-two years old. Dying wasn't on the agenda. I have too much stuff to do yet." I turned my frustration on a loose stone, punting it out into the darkness.

"I know what you mean. My to-do list isn't a quarter done. I'd like to think I'll get some more things crossed off."

He looked so pensive that it was all I could do not to go to him. I'd do the next best thing: I'd distract him and maybe learn something about him. "So, what's on your list?"

"I'd like to ski Vail for a season," he told me after a long pause. "Or Wapiti Creek. There's some amazing terrain up there." His wistful smile had me wishing to see it with him. I'd bet good money that he skied as well as he did everything else.

"A whole season?" I'd never been to a big resort even once. I mentally etched it on my own to-do list, especially if I somehow managed to get there with Kurt as my guide.

"Yeah, that's what I do in the off season. I do ski patrol at a resort. Sometimes I teach. Best thing to do in the mountains when there's snow." He smiled at some memory, but before I could ask him, he asked me, "What about you?"

I want to rip your clothes off and.... "I'd like to dive Vanuatu. Going to have to come up with some serious bucks for that." Diving was the one thing that had made me hesitate to come to Colorado: no reefs.

It seemed I'd finally managed to think of something Kurt didn't know about. "Where the hell is Vanuatu?"

"South Pacific. I've gone diving in the Caribbean twice, but this is a whole different thing." Being in Vanuatu sounded really good right now. Surrounded by water. With Kurt.

"I hear you. I want to climb the Dolomites that way. Italian Alps," Kurt clarified. "Hey, I'll teach you to climb if you'll teach me to dive."

"Sounds good," and it did, since it meant that we'd survive this mess. I hoped I'd be able to take him up on that. "Or maybe teach me to ski first."

"Could do that. Or I could teach you to cook first." I shook my head at him. That would be funnier some other time or place. He realized his joke had fallen flat, because he went on. "What else is on your to-do list?"

I considered my answer carefully. What did I want to do? "I've never eaten sushi. A guy should eat sushi at least once, right?" Until now, however, I never really wanted to.

"If I'd known that, we wouldn't have cooked the trout the other night. You could have had it raw."

"Didn't think of that." Did anybody even make trout sushi? If he was trying to keep it light, I'd play along. "But you didn't make rice. We'd need some rice."

"I'll have to take you to a restaurant for that. It's tough to make rice in the mountains." He sounded like he was seriously considering how to make sushi happen for me. "Water doesn't boil at the right temperature up here."

That made me think of heat. The surrounding rock somewhat insulated the cave—we weren't uncomfortably warm, even with the wind. I turned back to look out the mouth of the cave at the orange swaths and blobs in the night. Could cook a lot of stuff on that much heat. The wind had died a little with dark, but not much. At least it wasn't pointing straight into the cave. I heard footsteps come up behind me. For a guy who should be resting with the leg elevated, Kurt wasn't staying put very well. "I stuck my foot in it, didn't I?"

"No. Don't worry about it." There were a thousand other, worse things than that, dancing among the trees and brush. Hungry orange things that wanted the wood and our lives. But my life was mine, for these few hours; shouldn't I be able to spend it how I wanted? Or at least try? If I asked and Kurt said no, the humiliation might dog me the rest of my life, but it wouldn't be long. He might say yes. He might spend the rest of our time angry with me. Might take a swing at me. He might think I was a jerk, or he could laugh. I studied the fire, trying to find words that would make him say yes. I'd had my arm around him as I helped him travel the distance to the cave. He'd let me do his first aid. He had let me touch him out of necessity, but would he let me touch him out of desire? He had let me comfort him a little bit ago.

I wasn't sure what he was trying to see, but now Kurt stood next to me, helping me stand vigil.

Taking a deep breath and letting it out slowly, I took the biggest chance I'd ever taken before. "There has to be something else you want." I spoke without turning to look at him. If anger flashed behind his eyes, I didn't care to see it. He shifted slightly, first left, then right. Left again, away from me. Wrong way, Kurt. "Something you could even get without a plane ticket across an ocean or going forty miles into town."

"There is." He turned to me, but I couldn't look at him yet. His hand on my shoulder burned hotter than the fire—why was he touching me? "Jake, I want to suck your cock."

EIGHTEEN

Now I whipped around to stare at him with my mouth hanging open. Of all the things Kurt could have said, this was the one thing I both wanted the most and expected the least. He wanted me? He wanted sex with me? Maybe he just wanted the sex and I was the only one around? I didn't care—I'd take it. He'd been driving me mad for days, and now he offered to do what I wanted most? I had to struggle for the words, and he could say that?

I must have taken too long to think all these thoughts, because he took his hand away, leaving me cold and alone. His gaze dropped down and left, his face painfully vulnerable. "I'm sorry, forget it. I shouldn't have said anything. Sorry." He turned to retreat—maybe it hadn't been that easy to say.

"No!" I grabbed his shoulder and spun him around, pulling him into me. "Don't be sorry!" He plastered himself against me, the way I'd been dreaming, his mouth below mine. Then his mouth was pressed to my lips—I kissed him roughly, passionately responding to the invitation that dovetailed so perfectly with my deepest longings. Weeks of hiding and not knowing, of

wanting and not having, ruled me in that moment, my desire flaring hotter than anything outside our cave.

My hands gripped his upper arms; I felt him flex and nearly twist out of my grasp, but he wasn't tearing away. No, he had his arms around me, holding me as close as I gripped him. My cock responded before my brain did, filling to stiffness inside its denim prison.

"I thought—" he started, when I let him up for air, but I wouldn't let him speak.

"Don't talk!" I growled, and stopped his mouth again with mine. "Don't say anything!" My tongue ventured between his lips—he parted them to let me in.

"But—" he tried again a moment later, so I shushed him the best way I knew how. He sagged in my arms for a moment before standing tall and strong again, to return my kisses with equal force. Then he took the lead, pulling my lower lip into his mouth and sucking on it. I moaned as he tongued me, ferocious with passion, and I pulled him closer yet with a hand at the small of his back.

He was as hard as I was, as trapped inside clothing. That couldn't continue. My hand rested at his back—it was easy to grab the T-shirt and yank. I had it off him in one smooth movement once he realized what I was doing and let go that small amount that let me get it off him. More kisses would fortify me enough to release him again while he stripped me—only the reward of being skin to skin at last could loosen my grip. I'd dreamed of this, fantasized about this, touched myself over and over again while I imagined this—at last I crushed Kurt to my bare chest, with promises of so much more with every second. I had to squeeze him and run my hands over his naked back. The fabric over his ass was going to have go, too, but first I ran my hands over his utilities, then under. The cheeks I'd been thinking about were now in my hands. One muscular bun in each palm let me pull him tightly against me to feel his stiff cock against my own.

Kurt had his hand on the back of my head now, controlling the kiss, touching me. His other hand caressed my back, burning like fire, and then it slipped down my utilities. He gripped my ass the way I gripped his, and again I mirrored his motions. We played with each other's butts with our mouths crushed together, tasting of smoke and fear and potato chips, but tasting of ourselves and each other. Best taste in the world.

His cock rubbed against mine through the cloth; time to change that. Hands on his shoulders, I turned him around to press his back to my front while my mouth found his skin. His scent was intoxicating: smoke mixed with honest sweat, under-laid with maleness. The heady mix of taste and smell made me fumble as my hands searched for his fly. We got in each other's way trying to undo his belt and button, so I reached lower to rub his shaft while he undid the hardware. I had a free hand for one nipple; he liked this, I'd seen him do it, and rolling the hard peak in my fingers was the gentlest thing we were doing.

His cock sprang free, and it would have been easier to push his utilities down if I hadn't been grinding against him from the back, but my erection pushed up against his ass, his muscular ass that I'd watched walk away from me, and he was here close to me now. If we could just get these damned denim body condoms off, I'd be pressed against his crack.

It almost didn't matter, because he was free and jutting out from his clothing where I could touch him at last. With my cheek against his neck, I groped around—my fingers found him and closed around his shaft.

Hard and full in my hand, he was what I'd dreamed of every time I touched myself. He was nearly as long as I was, maybe seven inches, letting my hand move a familiar distance to stroke him. His uncut skin slipped farther than I was used to, over his glans and back. Without thought I began that stroking I'd done so often lately, only this time it was Kurt's cock I stroked, Kurt's soft skin travelling over hard shaft, and Kurt who was going to come from it.

"Slow down, Jake, slow down!" he gasped as he grabbed my hand to show me what he wanted. I'd try to do it his way, but I was so focused on the fulfillment of my dream that I had trouble surrendering control. The feeling of my length nestled into his ass didn't improve my ability to follow directions any, and when I licked the salt and sweat from his back, it was too much for both of us. I held still a moment too late: Kurt spurted and moaned his pleasure, his cock rippling in my grip. He shook with his spasms, leaning heavily against my arm across his chest. My own orgasm would have spilled over, too, but I jerked my hips away from him barely in time—two more thrusts against his butt would have done it. It would have been great, but what he'd offered would be better. Only that kept me from finishing.

As I pulled back from the brink, my mind cleared a little, enough to be aware of Kurt panting in his aftermath. I'd be his aspen tree at last. I turned him around to hold him slumped against me. His arms crept around my waist, his face pressed into my neck. He'd let me know when he was ready to go on. He'd come; I hoped he'd still want to continue. My unfulfilled flesh throbbed with need. The faint, orange light from outside made his skin glow. I stroked tracks into the sweat.

"Offer still stands," he mumbled into my neck a short time later. Tipping his face up for a kiss meant yes. The first desperation had left me, replaced with a more controlled yearning. I could be patient for the twenty seconds it would take to get me stripped.

We hopped him to the bear-shaped rock that had given me such a jolt earlier; it was the right height to lean my butt against. He kissed me with his hands on my fly, undoing me in every way. Slowly, too slowly, he drew the zipper down, then worked underwear and utilities down over my hips with his hands slipped under the layers. His tongue trailed over mine, and his hands helped my cock escape my clothes to bounce against his belly. I moaned as I touched his body with my cock for the very first time.

It must have taken twenty-one seconds because my patience was gone. Crushing him against me to kiss him hard brought my erect cock against his semi-erect one. Kurt gave as good as he got until he decided it was time to get on with it. He broke the kiss with his hands against my abs, pushing me backward until our mouths separated and my bare butt hit the rock. He had his back to the entrance of the cave, putting his face in shadow, but I could imagine the cheeky grin as he slowly lowered himself, his hands tight on my hips. The tip of my cock drew a line up him, and if it felt this good to touch his skin, what would his mouth be like? Maybe he was going this slow to pay me back for going too fast—he drew out the delicious agony of sliding against his cock, then his belly, then his chest.

It took damned near forever before Kurt knelt in front of me, hands on my hips, holding me still. Enough faintly orange light came into the cave to let me see his face lifted up to mine. I don't know if he could see my naked longing in the flickering light, but he must have known anyway because at last, at last, he took me in his mouth.

I never knew it would be this good.

Never knew what the velvety softness of an eager tongue

would be like, never knew what the heat of lips would be like, never knew what the slide against palate would be like. Never knew. Imagined, yeah, but the reality of Kurt far surpassed anything I'd fantasized. Now I knew. And there'd be no going back.

He took the head into his mouth enough to play with and tease as he slipped it in and out. His lips crinkled in a smile around my cock when I let out a long, shuddery moan, the only way I could tell him how wonderful it was, because there wasn't a molecule of oxygen left in the part of my brain that made words. "Ohhhh" must have told him plenty, because he came down farther onto my shaft now, a fraction of an inch with every stroke. His tongue swirled, wetting me—his lips slid over my skin as he took me bit by bit into his mouth. Now and then he'd come off me completely for breath, and I was bereft until wet warmth engulfed me again. One thing came to be crystal clear: this wasn't Kurt's first time. I couldn't think about that now.

I wasn't too sure what to do with my hands. I wanted to touch him, but I could only reach his head. Mindful that I'd already given him too much and brought him to orgasm too soon, I kept from touching him, because I might pull him down onto me farther than he wanted to go. Both hands on the rock would keep me from falling over because my knees were going to custard.

Kurt went from playing to serious now. One hand left my hip and gripped my straining shaft at the base, which still left a lot of room for his mouth. When he moved his mouth and his hand the same direction, it sent sparks through my body to pool in my groin, but I think he went too far, because he gagged and pulled back. Pumping me with his hand let him catch his breath, and now I could run my fingers through his short, blond hair without risking a choke.

"So good," were all the words I could form, but I wanted him to go back to what he was doing, oh I wanted to be in his mouth again. So good, amazingly good, mind blowing good. "Please," I managed, and he laughed.

"Fuck my mouth, Jake." Now he had two hands on my wet cock, stroking in unison, letting a couple of inches of head and shaft show when he pushed close to my groin. "Do it, fuck my mouth," and he slipped my cock back in, flicking madly with his tongue.

I'd been holding still, letting him pick the rhythms, but now I was sure I wouldn't choke him. I began to flex my hips, pushing as much of my cock as I could into his busy mouth, glad for the safety his hands afforded because I had to keep touching him. I thrust into his greedy, sucking mouth, screaming wordlessly. I wanted to do this endlessly; I wanted to climax. The way his tongue swiped over me, I would soon explode.

Burning gambel oak had nothing on me as I caught fire and detonated, spewing hot come in bursts and pops. He held me through my explosion, never taking his mouth from my shaft, holding tight against the waves pulsing through me. His hands were gentle but firm, holding me still; his mouth was gentle but firm, catching my climax. A last shudder went through me, and I stroked his hair to let him know I'd finished.

I had no idea he would do with his mouthful. I'd come to orgasm in the middle of a lot of groaning; it probably wasn't enough warning if he didn't want to taste.

With a last lick, he let me slip from his mouth. I kept my hands lightly on his head, ready to let him pull away if he needed to, but he stayed on his knees before me. When he swallowed, I brushed my fingers through his hair but did not dare to speak. I thought he might get up, but he leaned his forehead into the hollow of my groin, equally silently. He put his arms up on my thighs, hands on my waist. We stayed like that a long time, until he began to shift his knees uncomfortably. The rock bit into my butt, making it time to stand and bring him to his feet.

The salty tang of come met me with his kiss, just the one, gentler than any we'd already shared. We stood, embracing, in the dark cave, and for a time I was able to forget about the fire in the wonder of what we'd just done. His head rested on my shoulder, my cheek against his hair, when the world lit up.

NINETEEN

Our heads snapped around—thunder boomed before the lightning disappeared. Helluva of a way to break a reverie—I'd been to quieter reggae concerts. Might be able to hear what Kurt's voice again in a few minutes. I assumed he was saying, "Come on!" as he hobbled to the mouth of the cave. We stood looking over the scrubby oaks with night vision that only slowly returned, searching for anything new that had been set alight.

The sky was the darkest I'd seen since I came to the mountains. The sky, normally swept with stars, showed ugly gray and could have been mistaken for concrete. It wasn't all smoke, though that still flowed from the pine and oak torches. Lightning flared again, farther away this time, letting the thunder have half a second to catch up. The fire that had grown with the shifting winds was nearer now, an orange, mindless malevolence that crackled in the gambel oak. I'd almost believed the flare and crash had been the truck going up, but the spot where I knew it stood was still dark.

More lightning crazed the sky, showing the truck right where we'd left it. One more step back into the cave seemed like a good idea before the electrical charges built up enough for another blast. The dry storm that had threatened all day, pushed by unreliable winds, arrived to torment us with laden clouds that dropped nothing.

The night was magnificent, it was inimical, it would kill us and never know. The danger from the fire matched the danger from the skies that crashed and flickered, leaving afterimages swimming with streaks. We could only watch the heavens battle the flaming land and feel small.

I felt a little less small when I stepped behind Kurt to wrap my arms around his chest. I pulled him farther into the cave, having no other way to keep him safe from the night. He stepped back against me and put both hands on my forearms, clinging tightly. Together we watched the elements, our heads touching, saying nothing, though we groaned when the truck took a direct hit.

The wind changed again, the damned wind that couldn't make up its mind, coming straight against the scarp and our refuge. The sandblasting sent us both dashing for our clothing, the fire jackets being the best protection against the debris, but currents changed yet again before we got all the way into the clammy sleeves.

The night itself changed when another brilliant bolt of lightning struck practically on our doorstep. The thunder pealed and didn't die away—it shifted to a low hissing that made me shake my head as if I could dislodge the noise. Not the crackle of fire, not thunder: it wasn't any noise that I could comprehend, until Kurt dropped his jacket and began to hop and whoop.

"It's raining! Oh, my Lord, it's raining!"

Together we dashed the few steps to the mouth of the cave, where we leaned out into the night to taste the blessed water falling from the heavens. Hands out into the torrents that were only now released, we touched splashes of hope.

The rain attacked the flames, making the night hiss. If the wind carried the rain drops sideways from one fiery branch, they would only collide with another. The vanguard drops turned to steam before they hit, but as the storm continued, the water came closer and closer to actually touching, then sizzled away on the hot wood until at last the forest began to moisten.

The rains came down, down, down, for time untold—the fire struggled to breathe against the wetness. Kurt and I stood, faces to the rain, watching the orange flames dwindle to flickers and then to red glows in the night. Still the rains came. We edged as close to the brink as we could. We'd have left the cave completely and done the rain dance on the ground, but the lightning kept us cautious as it lit up the sky.

Enough rain fell into our hands that we could scrub our faces, the dirt scraping as we washed it away. Wet hands against skin took off layers of smoke and sweat after the boots and the utilities came completely off at last. Kurt's hands ran down my back and sides as the rainwater poured over us; mine roamed over him, cleaning him and touching him. We'd break off scrubbing from time to time to hold each other tightly—to warm up, not merely to embrace. The hugs warmed my heart but not my groin because this natural cold shower was making my teeth chatter.

"Your lips taste blue," Kurt told me after hours of storm. "Let's go in."

"Let's dry off with one shirt," I suggested. "Then we can wear the rest of the clothes." I planned to dry him with mine because he had less insulation than I did and needed some clothing.

"Nope, going to sleep next to you naked," Kurt told me

with a smile in his voice that got swallowed by the yawn. That was just fine with me. I suddenly realized that I was cold, hungry, and exhausted. Happier than I'd ever been, though, because I was going to sleep next to Kurt and live to wake up again. We opened the fire shelter on top of a layer of fire pants to pad the rocky cave floor, then crawled in. The nasty wet jackets couldn't come inside. We draped them over the fire shelter and hoped they wouldn't slide off while we slept. It made a tight fit, the two of us in a one man shelter that wasn't much bigger than a sleeping bag anyway, but we cuddled up with much wiggling, knowing that turning over wasn't going to happen. I lay spooned against his back, my arm over his chest, my lips near his ear.

"Good night," Kurt told me as he'd said every night since we moved into the cabin.

"Good night," I told him as I'd replied every night before. Tonight was different, though, because he kissed me.

TWENTY

It had been well into the wee hours when we finally went to sleep, and I still woke up early. Another four hours of sack time sounded really good, but only if I could turn over. Holding my sleeping partner offered the only consolation for being stuck on my right side on a cold rock slab. His chest moved gently under my arm as I watched him sleep and thought about how much I'd wanted this very thing. Naked and snugged up against him, I could wake him with a kiss, or....

He might be as stiff as I was. My cock was as stiff as my muscles. While I might be hard and raring to go, my body might not be able to move enough to thrust against him without a good long stretch. I was ready for more sex now that we'd gotten past the barrier of the first time. His ass and my cock were crushed together—it would be a few inches' motion to go from close to inside. And Lord, how I wanted that. If his mouth on me felt like heaven, how much more so his body?

A few inches and a liberal application of something slippery. I knew enough to not even try without lube, and now that he'd seen me, Kurt might not want to do that at all. He'd had both hands full with some left over for his mouth. I'd measured, every guy has, and would almost eight inches long and close to five inches around even fit in such a nice tight place? So far, Kurt had the answers. This time I'd have to ask the question.

I'd turn over for him, if he wanted. I'd held his hard cock last night; I wanted the opportunity to taste him the way he'd tasted me. I wanted to feel him inside me, moving, thrusting. Make him call my name. I was a little scared to try it, but trusted Kurt enough to know he wouldn't hurt me intentionally. Wonder what we could use for lube.

I'd crammed the small first aid kit inside my jacket pocket yesterday. Kurt and I radiated enough heat that we stayed warm even though the jackets slid off while we slept. Mine had fallen to the side I could reach, letting me fumble the kit out. My right arm lay trapped under me, so I had to unzip the pouch with my teeth, and I was clumsy enough that I dumped the contents all over Kurt. He woke to a shower of Band-Aids in his ear.

"What are you doing?" He brushed the packet of burn cream off his cheek. Hmm, that might work.

"Looking for ointment?"

That got a puzzled laugh. "Let's see where it went. First, let's get out of this tinfoil sarcophagus, because I can't feel my right side."

He opened the flap the rest of the way and rolled out, groaning. He made it to his feet without favoring the injury.

"How's the ankle?" I asked, since he had both feet down on the ground.

"A lot better. I think it works again." He rolled the foot, experimenting.

Watching him stretch aroused me; I rolled to my back to let him get a look once he'd put his arms down, but he headed to the mouth of the cave, limping only a little. I stuck my head out of the shelter. Purely to observe. Right? The view from the back was fine indeed.

The sound effects weren't so fine, though, because I could hear Max's voice yelling, "You can't put the fire out that way, Carlson!"

I have never scrambled into clothes so fast in my life.

The banter at the mouth of the cave continued while I dressed, good-natured nonsense between old friends. That Kurt could carry this sort of thing on while being caught damned near *en flagrante* made me wonder if either he didn't care or if he was that good of an actor. Thinking back to the other night, I recalled he hadn't panicked when he'd had a knife at his face. I should quit panicking, too. The banter went from yelling to conversational tones, as if Max drew nearer with every word.

"Ho, Max!" I called, coming to the mouth of the cave with a boot in my hand. "What brings you out this way?" We didn't have to act like we'd been caught circle jerking—we had a legitimate reason to be out here that also happened to include reasons to be buck naked. Kurt headed into the cave to dress. Max had brought the perfect excuse for me to be uneasy; he led two saddle horses and a pack horse. Most of what I knew about horses was that one end kicked and the other end bit.

Max's yellow slicker partially covered the brown and white paint horse he rode, making a polyethylene centaur of them. The rain drops beaded on him, making drippy trails to fall at the horse's feet. No longer falling in sheets like last night, the rain came down in a normal summer shower. "I'm the cavalry, come charging over the hill. Since I'm the only one besides you who knows where this place is exactly."

Still, I was surprised that the Chief hadn't sent one of the other crews in a truck for both assessing the fire and collecting us. "Rich and Abigail would have parked by our truck and leaned on the horn until we showed up," I pointed out.

"They could have been honking a while, but they're over on the other fire line. The lightning started another blaze on the other side of Meeker. Everybody else is on that crew, since the Chief thought LandSat on this site looked pretty good. So I volunteered." Not even Max called the Chief "Harold."

"Glad to see you and the horses too. We humped the equipment over here on foot." Kurt returned to the mouth of the cave, fully clothed and with a tank in each hand. "Could have been a long walk out."

"Didn't know what you'd have, that's why I brought the pack horse." The animal shifted uneasily as Max dismounted, making me think he didn't like the rain or the scent of wet ashes.

"Not all that much. Come on, Jake, let's get the shelter folded." Did I hear a tinge of regret in his voice? Kurt brought the axes up and handed them to Max, who started to attach them to the harness. We returned to the silver cocoon, where we collapsed the thing back into its tank-like shape and wrestled it into the bag. Kurt's eyes met mine, silently conveying a message. Only, I couldn't figure out if he meant "Don't you dare tell" or "Hold that thought for later." Whatever the message, the heat in his gaze caused strange flutterings in my stomach that had nothing to do with physical hunger or the smooshed sandwiches we'd wolfed down the night before.

As badly as I wanted out of that cave, I think I'd have given pretty much anything for one more hour alone with Kurt. The one time I wished he wasn't so danged efficient, he made short work of ending our stay at Motel Slate. Everything got packed up and carried out. We left no trace in that cave, no sign that my life had been altered forever in there. The bear rock looked no different—only I had changed. I didn't know about Kurt; we had no chance to talk. And with Max around, who amounted to the local "all news, all the time" network, the immediate future didn't look too promising for a heart-to-heart either.

Max tied the last strap as I jumped down off the ledge. I expected Kurt to hop down, too, before remembering his injured ankle. "Hand on my shoulder, Kurt."

"Hah." He sat down and prepared to slide down the scarp.

"Be macho some other time. You need both feet to ride. Or —" I had an idea that might goad Kurt's pride into making him behave. "Max, can we strap him across the pack horse like a rolled-up rug?"

"We could." Max eyed Kurt appraisingly. "Do it his way, Carlson. The Chief told me you'd been hurt. Or no breakfast for you."

"It's a lot better," Kurt argued, but he did slide down with my help. Was touching me again, even for a reason so innocent, that bad of a prospect?

"Food, anyone?" Max produced shiny cylinders from his pack. "I brought sausage and egg burritos, with my notorious green chile."

"Yum!" Kurt reached for his. I unwrapped foil to get at the good stuff inside, thinking of last night, knowing I had better not watch Kurt put something like a burrito in his mouth or I'd lose it completely. Should have turned so he didn't have to watch me eat, because Max had to pound his back before he choked completely.

"Slow down, buddy," Max admonished him, and this time I choked.

"What's with you two?" Max said as he thumped me between the shoulder blades.

"Unfamiliarity with the concept of food," Kurt told him.

"Lunch should have been about twenty-four hours ago." He demolished the burrito, crumpled the foil, and placed it in his pocket. Then he patted his belly and belched in appreciation. "That was good, thanks." Now that we probably wouldn't starve, Kurt returned to firefighter mode. "Think we should check the truck first, check in with the Chief."

We put the fire suits on again. Hot, sticky, stinky suits that felt like they weighed a ton. They would be our protection against the rain, and we'd need them for scouting the fire site where we wouldn't take the horses, but I wished we could do without them. And Max. Gratitude for the food only went so far.

Once we reached the truck, our good intentions fizzled. The two-way radio refused to so much as buzz.

"Think the engine will even turn over, or did the lightning fry the entire electrical system?" I inspected the truck, trying to see where grounding might have occurred. A gambel oak branch showed charring and didn't quite touch the front fender. It probably had been long enough last night.

Kurt came to examine the crisped limb. "Guess your wet line paid off, Jake. That could have taken out the truck."

"Thanks." I squirmed inside my heavy fire suit, the praise from Mr. Competent feeling better than any *A* on a test. After the reality of the last twenty-four hours, I wondered why school had ever been something to worry about. Life was pass/fail, and we'd survived the night with at least some of our equipment intact. Guess I'd helped us pass.

Max reminded us he was there. "Don't try the engine—the electrical system could start a fire. It needs to be inspected first."

"No point. The pinion gear is gone. This puppy isn't moving." Kurt slapped the tanker. "Back on your horse, cowboy."

Very funny. I hadn't ridden in years. Summer camp a decade back hadn't given me but a few hours of experience, and no helpful wrangler held the bridle this time. Getting on was a trial; the beast sidestepped with me hopping after it, one foot in the stirrup, trying to get enough leverage to swing my leg over. I couldn't get on, I couldn't get all the way off, and I might have had to hop all the way to Rendezvous Lake Lodge if Max hadn't come to my rescue by grabbing the reins.

"There's a reason I'm not on one of the horseback teams," I told my companions as my face burned, as though my obvious ineptitude couldn't clue them in. The ground was a long way down, and the way my mount swiveled his ears back at me, I might be traveling that distance. Soon. Of course, Kurt sat confidently astride his mount, looking for all the world like a firefighting John Wayne, so grabbing the saddle horn wasn't an option. He had asked Max for a big leg up, out of respect for the ankle, which made me feel only marginally better.

"It's a skill, like any other," Max reassured me. "You can learn." He looked like he'd been born on a horse.

I'd have to learn fast; we had miles to go to reach the lodge.

We scouted the burned areas for any pockets of live flame and determined if smoldering areas posed a threat. Enough places needed our attention that the shortcut wasn't any faster than taking the long way. What would have been thirty miles by road amounted to about twelve miles by horseback, twelve long miles that turned my thighs to rubber, punctuated by a bit of shoveling and the occasional stomping. Max stayed with us and helped with the work. I thought the lodge needed tending, and I sure needed privacy to talk to Kurt, so I asked him why.

"Jake, this is the first day off I've had in two weeks," he replied with a wry grin. "I live and work in Paradise, and I never get to just enjoy it. A day on horseback with friends feels pretty good to me. And Kurt needs more help mounting than you can give him." He could have added "And because Kurt won't be able to help you if you topple off the horse and it runs away, which looks entirely possible," but he didn't.

Okay, I couldn't chase him off. I wanted to, though, because every single time I got my nerve up to talk to Kurt about the previous night, Max moved into earshot. Hiking back to town the long way with full gear would almost have been preferable to this. I had to ask Kurt "What next?" before I went completely berserk. Not even the promise of a hot shower in the bunkhouse when we got back to the lodge made me like Max's company one bit more right then.

There were plenty of opportunities to master mounting and dismounting as we dealt with a few pockets of coals, but for the most part, nature controlled the fire for us, though now a mere drizzle made up the bucket brigade. I was grateful, because I had envisioned the whole mountainside burnt black to the base of the scarp. "It will recover," Kurt told me as we walked the horses back to the lodge. "Some species even need the fire to reproduce, because the cones don't open to let the seeds out without heat." He pointed at a pinecone whose scales had flared widely, when I was used to seeing them furled up tight.

That thought gave me pause. In the past few weeks, I'd come to see how dangerous and destructive wildfire could be, and yet, out of destruction came rebirth. I wondered if the same would happen to me, or if, like the candled pines from yesterday, the burning might prove permanent.

The rain stopped a few miles past the burn zone, so I had another bit of practice getting on and off that blasted horse. This time, I wrapped the reins around the saddle horn enough to keep him in one place when I remounted after shedding the fire clothing, which I tied onto the pack horse. Kurt nodded approvingly. "You're getting it."

Riding was just one more skill that Kurt had perfected; he sat the horse easily and offered a little coaching.

"These boots aren't right for riding, but we're stuck with them. Try to keep the balls of your feet on the stirrups." Kurt and the horse both winced as my foot came out of one stirrup. "You might only get your toes in, but it works on your balance."

Before we got back to the lodge, the horse had concluded that I was there for the duration, even if I had all the grace of a sack of potatoes. He'd turn around periodically with "What? You're still there?" written all over his long, horsey face, and yes, I was.

When the temptation to grab the saddle horn had dwindled to once every five minutes, I had more leisure to think. "Why aren't you riding a mounted patrol?" I asked Kurt when we were in sight of the stables.

"I rode the last two years. It was time for a change." And the Chief had made Kurt stick with his change, even though Kurt had taken one look at me and tried to bolt.

The contrast between the way he handled a horse and the way he handled the tanker ate at me, and it was the only bit of curiosity I could indulge in with Max around. When we arrived at the corral, I commented, "I'm surprised the Chief let you switch from a horse team. You're good." He'd controlled his horse expertly when a rabbit jumped up under its hooves. My horse had bounced sympathetically, and the best that can be said is that I didn't fall off.

"Jake, I grew up riding and skiing, and after all these years, it's time to do them both so they're fun. I want to drive a truck for a while." He swung off the horse and wrapped the reins around the fence rail. End of discussion.

I'd flipped the stirrup over the seat to get at the girths under Max's watchful eye when a tiny woman in a blue chambray shirt and jeans came up to the fence. "I'm glad you guys are here. The Chief called about two hours ago. And again about an hour ago. And I think the phone's ringing again. You better go reassure him you aren't crispy critters."

Max shooed me away and solved the next problem. "Kurt and I will unsaddle for you. Go call him. Carlene, let him into my office to use the phone."

Following the woman back to the main lodge, I had a sneaky suspicion that Max had enough of the novice handling his horse. The novice certainly had enough of riding the horse. I hurt. Cowboys must toughen up after a while, because I never saw one totter around like this. My butt felt like hamburger, and my thighs might never come together again.

The man I spoke to didn't sound all that anxious, at least once I'd identified myself. The Chief wanted to get us out to the other fire site right away. "We need you boys out here with the hotshots, Jake. The fire is headed toward town," he told me when I called in. I didn't know how to judge the severity of the blaze when the hotshots, who were the real firefighters of the Forest Service, needed rangers as backup, but assumed it was, or could be, bad. He then asked, "How is Kurt's ankle?"

"He's walking with a limp, but he rode in without a problem." Kurt got irritated any time Max or I inquired, though he'd swallowed some more ibuprofen when he thought I wasn't looking.

"I can put him on command post. He can free up an able-bodied man. Jake, I'm glad we got you both back." The Chief's voice suddenly sounded like an arm around my shoulder.

"Good job on getting your wounded partner out." Somehow I knew he'd put men ahead of equipment. And that he wouldn't say one extra word about it. "How soon can you be here?"

"I don't know. We came in on horseback with Max. We'll have to find a ride." No one would come to fetch us when it meant taking hands off the fire line.

"Find one and get out here, Jake. The woods are burning." With that, he left me. Great.

"How do we get out to the fire site?" I asked Carlene. I loved her dearly already for not making calf eyes at either me or my partner. She could definitely teach the Meeker girls a thing or two. "Know anyone who'd give us a ride?" Maybe Max would lend us wheels, or someone headed to town wouldn't mind dragging a couple of rangers and gear along.

"You come with me," she said. "I'm going into town after the mail and the food order, and the Lodge kitchen is sending a big pot of chili for the firefighters."

"Great! Kurt and I will do a quick clean up and we'll be ready to go!" I wanted that shower, even if the clothes I wore were all I had with me.

"No, you won't, and I'm punishing myself for saying that, but that food truck won't wait, and the kitchen can't wait until it gets back around from Grand Junction." She wrinkled her nose at me. "We'll keep the windows open, and maybe I won't be able to tell you guys apart from the smoke in the air. You can hold the chili for me." Okay, so Carlene lost a few "lovable" points. With chili in the offing, however, she stood a good chance of gaining them back.

On the way to the pickup truck, Carlene, the chili, and I met Kurt hobbling up from the barn. "Where's the gear? We need to load it," I told him.

"No shower?" His face fell.

"We're loading now. The Chief wants us pronto, and Carlene is kind enough to haul us out there, but she's got a schedule to keep." I motioned with the pot of chili. "Dinner will be good, though."

Once in the truck, Kurt and I juggled the pot as we tried to find places for four long legs. Carlene had the seat pulled up enough to reach the pedals, cramping us considerably. I finally stuck my feet in Kurt's foot well, resting my thigh against his, which suited me just fine, until Carlene had to notice it out loud.

"What have you been doing to the poor boy, Kurt?" she teased. "Nobody saw you guys for days, and when we get you back, you're all snuggly and you're both walking funny."

"You're short, I'm hurt, and he just got off his first horse in ten years." Kurt's voice held a distinct chill. It was all true, and he could be telling her to back off because she was out of line... or maybe because I'd already gotten everything I was ever going to get.

Damn it, it was nobody's business but ours, even though nothing we'd done yet would account for my gait. Maybe later we'd have that issue. I pulled my thigh away, but we were so close to the dashboard that there was nowhere to pull to. I slopped some chili out, trying to find a couple of non-existent square inches.

"Sorry, that was tasteless," she said, chastened. "I didn't realize Jake was such a greenhorn." She adjusted the bench seat to give us a few more inches and sat up at the edge.

It didn't matter. Kurt pulled farther toward the door and stared out the window, lips pulled into a thin line. I didn't know what to do. What I wanted was to put my leg right back where it had been, but Carlene didn't need to know our business.

Especially when I didn't know what our business was. Kurt and I really needed to talk.

The Lodge's chili and two extra sets of hands were about equally well received. The other rangers and the hotshots were happy to see us: there was plenty of wind-driven flame to go around. The dry storm had set a dandy blaze here, and they hadn't gotten the rain we had. The lightning strike had gone undiscovered for about twelve hours, giving the fire a big head start.

Worst of all, with so many people constantly underfoot, I barely saw Kurt, let alone found a chance to talk to him. Every now and then, though, I'd catch a glimpse of another firefighter through the trees, head tipped back to drink from his canteen or wipe the sweat from his brow, and for a moment I'd think I was seeing Kurt. Command central lay behind the fire lines, and Kurt was only a voice on a radio, saying nothing that he couldn't say to every other man wielding a shovel or an axe.

For the next day and a half, we chopped, dug, cursed, and sweated, until the fire was adequately contained and the Chief started sending people home.

"Rich, Abigail, you can drop Jake up at his cabin on your way," the Chief said. "Jake, you'll do fire watch as best you can with the binoculars. Call anything in if you find it. And Rich, you two will patrol farther into Jake's section until we get the truck repaired. Kurt can work down here and then take it back up."

There had been no time to talk with Kurt on the fire line and there was no goodbye now. I nodded, and he nodded back, saying, "See you soon," leaving me to get into the tanker with a couple who would be sleeping together tonight. I tried not to hate them.

This would have been my big opportunity to get to know

them better, if I'd felt like talking, but I'd just left the man I desperately needed to talk to back on the fire line. Every minute headed the wrong direction threw another dry branch into my gut, where it burned with acid flame.

Abigail, who at five foot eight was the shortest, got the center of the big bench seat and the task of staying out of the way of the gearshift. Every time Rich shifted the manual transmission, she had to spread her knees to avoid getting whacked, and the soft murmurs and laughter they shared were probably salacious couple jokes. I tried not to listen, and I didn't want to know—I could imagine. I wanted jokes like that with Kurt.

They seemed to sense that I didn't want to talk, or maybe the way I snarled when they tried to ask about the fire Kurt and I had fought alone clued them in. I did apologize and told them what they needed to know about the lightning storm and the rain, but we spent twenty miles of silence after that. Maybe they thought my brush with death had left me shaken.

We did finally start to talk about halfway home, after we hit a bump in the road that lifted us off the seat. Something flashed at Abigail's throat as she bounced back to the seat: her engagement ring hung on a chain around her neck. It finally penetrated my thick head that here were the two people most likely to know about a ranger team getting along with sex involved. Whether or not they'd be upset if the rangers were both male wasn't a question I planned to explore. Neither Meeker nor Pueblo, Rich's home town, were known as bastions of openmindedness on the subject.

I nodded toward Abigail. "When is the wedding?"

She reached up to play with the dangling jewelry, sliding her third finger into it, chain and all. To wear it on her hand invited injury, the Chief explained back during orientation. He'd refused to give her the keys to their tanker until she showed him her impromptu necklace and satisfied him that love wouldn't break her fingers. "December. We'll need some time after the fire season ends to put it all together. It'll take weeks to make the dresses and all that." I tried to imagine the tomboy currently clad in ranger green utilities and smudges decked out in wedding white with a pouffy train and veil.

Rich laughed. "All I have to do is show up, relatively sober."

Abigail whacked his arm, ignoring his playful yelp. "You'll have a to-do list, buster!"

"Is anyone giving you grief about living together?" What was taken as a matter of course in bigger communities probably didn't fly very well in a place as small as Meeker. This might be my only way to sneak up on what I needed to know.

"Hah! Everyone! My dad tried to get the Chief to reassign us, even, or drop me from the crew completely. Old dinosaur with old dinosaur attitudes. You'd think if anyone would be for it, it would be him and Mom." Abigail wrinkled up her brow, while Rich blew air out between pursed lips. Guess he was destined for some interesting relationships with the in-laws. "They sure didn't know each other well enough before they got married, or they never would have done it."

"Abigail's mom lives over in Glenwood Springs now, and I don't think it's enough miles between them," Rich put in.

"What I figure is that if Rich and I do a ranger season together and I don't kill him before the end, we'll have a long and happy life together." Abigail patted Rich's thigh, a smug little smile playing on her lips.

"How is it working so far?" Now we were getting someplace.

"Pretty good. I say 'yes, dear' a lot." Richard lifted a hand from the steering wheel to rub his mouth. His tone of voice revealed everything that raised hand tried to hide.

"Only when I ask you for something you already plan to do, you—you—you *man*!" Abigail didn't sound particularly annoyed with him. I concluded that it was working fairly well.

"You might decide to throw me back. The season is young." Rich didn't look very concerned about the possibility.

"That would trigger a feeding frenzy among the local girls." I had a sudden vision of Lindy, Tanya, and Dawn with big shark teeth, circling around Rich.

Abigail and Rich both laughed, but she sounded amused, and he was acknowledging a real and present danger. "I put a ring on Abigail to get Tanya to back off." She thumped his thigh with the side of her fist. "Among other reasons." She stroked the thumped spot. Could Kurt and I ever touch each other so casually in company? First we had to work out the touching each other in private part. That is, if Kurt ever even *wanted* to touch me again.

"Tanya seems to have set her sights on Kurt," I said, thinking back to our trip to town. I hadn't met her, although I feared coming back to the cabin to find her and Lindy hanging curtains.

"She's been chasing him for the last two years. They all have." Abigail looked toward me then with something in her eyes that might have been sympathy. "Though some of them will start chasing you. They're fickle that way, and a bit tired of Kurt brushing them off."

"Lindy already has." Next week's grocery trip would be an exercise in diplomacy; I didn't plan to get caught. That "Kurt brushing them off" warranted more thought—later.

Abigail considered this. "You could do worse. She's sweet." Abigail had probably known Lindy since they were small. "But she won't be the only one. Rangers are popular guys."

"Yeah," Rich agreed, making me think his bachelor days had

been entertaining, especially after Abigail frowned at him. Well, good for him. "So far, nobody has caught Kurt, though everybody tries."

"Not 'everybody'," Abigail objected.

"No, sweetheart, not everybody." He grinned at her, and it was plain that willowy, brunette Abigail and tall, lanky Rich had eyes for no one but each other, though I reminded Rich to have eyes for the road. Our turnoff was coming up.

"Still, he hasn't dated anyone, exactly. He's just friendly to everyone," Abigail went on. "From something he said, I think he got his heart broken before he got here, and it's taking a long time to heal. He never talks about her. Never."

Maybe, maybe it had been a him?

Two seasons of pursuit, and none of the local girls had captured Kurt. I thought back to the enormous trout I'd caught without planning to, and a spark of hope grew that I could capture the larger, more desirable prize. He'd been in my arms briefly—I'd do everything in my power to see that this big one didn't get away.

They dropped me off at the cabin, which was both home and a totally strange place. Without Kurt, it was nothing but a shack in the wilderness.

As I offloaded my gear, Abigail caught me for a quiet word. "Jake, Kurt would want you to have this." She kissed me lightly on the cheek, making me gawp at her. Oh dear Lord! I stood frozen, staring at her with wide eyes. She couldn't... I didn't... Kurt didn't... how the hell could she know?

"He would?" I asked, my heart pounding a frantic beat. I didn't know how she could have known that. Even if she was right, privacy didn't exist on the line. Had he told her? Told her what? When? Suddenly I wanted to grab her and shake out every single word Kurt had ever said to her. Only, Rich might take offense to that and kick my ass.

"He'd want you to be sure we're all glad you guys made it." She kissed my cheek again, then turned to make a face at Rich, who'd honked the horn on the second smooch. "Jake, don't hurt him." Then she got back in the truck, leaving me to wonder just which way she meant that, how much she actually knew, and if our secret would be safe with her.

TWENTY-ONE

If I continued to sit at the top of the ridge, scanning for fires in a big circle, I'd lose my mind in short order. The restlessness overwhelmed me every time I thought of us in the cave, whether I recalled Kurt's cock in my hand, mine in his mouth, or holding on to him, watching the creeping flames. I wanted to touch him again in every way, I needed to feel his body against mine, and I was desperately afraid Kurt didn't want the same.

Round and round my head, thoughts chased each other. What would I do? Where would I go? While running had sounded good a few days ago, now I thought I'd rather have teeth pulled.

Don't hurt him. Abigail's words rang in my head. She meant well, and she'd known Kurt longer than I had, maybe, but how well did she really know him? Well enough to speak for him? I didn't want to hurt him; I wanted to believe that night was more than the product of fear and impending death. I didn't want to be the last novelty before oblivion.

If that was all it would be, I'd have to live with it. Not sure how but, worst case scenario, maybe leaving would be best after all.

Don't hurt him. Did she mean that if he made a pass, I should accept it, or at least not punch his lights out? Did she know something I didn't about how close Kurt liked to get to his partners? This was his third season with the Forest Service. Did he make a habit of seducing his wingman? How or why would Abigail know?

If I was one in a long list, there wasn't a damned thing I could do about it. Maybe he'd keep me until the end of the season.

"Don't hurt him," she'd said. What about him hurting me?

I spent a lot of time running from the ridge to the archery range. I'd scan the surrounding terrain, then run back down to shoot another three quivers' worth of arrows. The quiver had eleven arrows in it after Motorbike Boy rode off with number twelve, now slightly bent and useless for shooting but proudly displayed on the cabin wall. Trying to remember everything Kurt had coached me about shooting kept my mind off other things, sort of. The aspen tree and I had two interludes on that first day back, in between firing and fetching arrows.

My aim improved, even if my mental health didn't. Kurt and I had shared the archery before the fire; we could at least have that after, no matter what. Without him nearby, I could concentrate as I never had before. I had to be good at this, for Kurt, for us, and for my own self-respect. I shot the last quiver with every arrow in the target, and two in the red, stopping only when my hand hurt too much to draw another bowstring.

Dinner wasn't much fun. I didn't have the heart to cook something, or even run back and forth to the bear box and the lake for some variety. A lonely peanut butter sandwich at the bear box, where all the ingredients were and I didn't have to pretend to eat it for any enjoyment, became the wilderness equivalent of eating over the sink. I might have brought it back to the table and tried to read one of the library books, but I'd already looked at the short stories and thrown the book back into the cabin, frustrated and unable to concentrate.

I ended up at the lake after my last run up the ridge with the binoculars. Nothing burned that I could see, so I went to what I guess was my happy place here. The fish were safe from me tonight, unless they got conked on the head with the rocks I skipped. The *plink, plink, plink* of the stones across the lake soothed my frazzled nerves. Probably the water level changed by two inches from all the rocks that went to the bottom. I did finally drag the fridge box up for a drink of milk straight from the carton. The milk was still good after several days. I'd have to tell Kurt that our new fridge worked. One of many things I longed to tell him.

The sun had gone down. My day was over, but the empty cabin didn't welcome me. It wasn't home tonight. Tossing and turning wouldn't disturb anyone tonight. No soft breathing from across the room would tell me all was right with the world. I lay in my sleeping bag, but there was no comfortable position in that cot, no matter how I searched for it.

There might be a comfortable spot across the room. Silently I padded over to Kurt's cot to zip myself into his bag, and only then could I fall asleep.

TWENTY-TWO

I woke to the scent of Kurt's shaving cream, which clung to the flannel lining of the bag and to the pillow. Lying on my back with the pillow clasped to my chest, I thought again of the man who usually slept here.

All the overtures had been Kurt's. All the moments of casual nudity in the last week had been his, at least initially. Had he been offering himself all along and I'd just been too stupid to realize it?

Too good to be true, I decided as I got up, leaving the bag unzipped and rumpled, which matched the one on my cot. We were scared, he was thinking of his lost mother, he needed some comfort, that's all, and I was the only one there. Maybe he thought I couldn't respond to anything other than sex, although I didn't think of myself as that heartless. Did he? I had at least fifteen reasons stored up for why he wouldn't want any part of me once he returned to the cabin, and why one of us wouldn't remain there once he returned.

It would probably be me to leave, I thought glumly on the climb up the path to the ridge with a water bottle and binoculars. He was the more experienced ranger; he knew what he was doing. I was the newbie, the liability. I had somewhere to go, a backup plan that started in early September. If I called the School of Pharmacy and told them that I wouldn't be deferring entrance after all, that I'd be there this year and not next, as I'd thought, Kurt could keep his job and livelihood, and I'd only miss out on the year of freedom from academics that I'd hoped for.

It would put miles between us, if he didn't want to look at me again to remember what we'd done in a cave while waiting to die young.

By my second trip down from the ridge to the archery range, I had amassed another set of reasons that would keep me there in the cabin, with my lover by my side. Kurt, my lover— oh, those words sounded good. I wanted to hold him again, to touch him and explore him, to find out where the ticklish spots were and the ones that made him moan. He'd offered, he'd enjoyed, he'd touched me. He kissed me. Didn't that mean more than anything else? If it was nothing but comfort sex with a fellow ranger in a time of peril, he didn't have to kiss me. He could have just dropped my trousers and done what he suggested. Wiped his mouth and gone back to watching the fire, maybe holding tight to me for the illusion of safety in numbers. But he kissed me, hard and completely. If I closed my eyes and thought hard enough, I could still feel his lips on mine.

No, I had been the one to kiss him. He hadn't seduced me —he had offered to blow me. He had only kissed back, and I had better never expect that to happen again, short of the woods burning down around us.

The sad, bad thoughts chased me up and down the hill from ridge to range. More than once I turned the binoculars to our road, hoping to see our battered old tanker grumbling down the track, but knowing that the mechanics had probably only gotten the differential opened up. The busted pinion gear would probably need parts brought in from Grand Junction, if not freighted in from Denver. It would be a while yet before I saw Kurt again, before this horrible dilemma could be resolved.

A few good thoughts pursued me too. He might have meant it. He might not have known where to start, any more than I did, and so he started in the only place that he thought I would start, by offering benefits to a friend. If that was all he wanted, I might have to leave for pharmacy school after all, because I didn't think I could stand being just another activity, an alternative to fishing or archery. "It's raining, so drop your drawers." Or maybe I could, if that was all I could have. Banter in the day, boffing at night, just to stave off the boredom. He hadn't made me any promises. The good thoughts went sour really fast when I thought of it like that.

The way to his heart might be with six inches of steel, if he came back with "Oopsy, let's just forget that ever happened." That thought brought me to a halt halfway down the path. I didn't want to forget, I didn't want to ignore it, I didn't want to put aside the most amazing experience of my life. Kurt wouldn't do that to me. He couldn't do that to me. If he did, I still couldn't attack him, though his words would be steel plunged into my own heart.

I could live with "It was great, but let's not do it again." I'd just have to be miles away from him to live like that, because I could never look at him again and not remember how it felt to touch him.

The way to his heart might be through being as hypercompetent as he was. I sighted the arrows at the target, loosing them one at a time, and retrieved all of them from one ring or another; not a one had missed. My cluster had shrunk, exactly like he promised. I stowed the arrows and the bow in the cabin for the night. Seven trips up the ridge and seven trips down to the range had eaten up most of my daylight.

I wanted little jokes and single words that told an entire story just to us. "Bear" would be one. "RAV4" might be another. "Beans." That made my stomach rumble, which sent me to the bear box. Cooking anything was beyond my initiative. I slapped together another peanut butter sandwich.

I had a little light and nothing to do with it, so I took my rod and tackle box down to the lake. The evening sky was going a deeper blue with streaks of clouds at the horizon. The evening star would be coming up soon, as would the moon, but for now it was not yet twilight, something that didn't exist long in the mountains. A cloud of gnats danced over a shallow, rocky area near the shore where the big trout came to feed.

A small, hairy fly seemed about right, so I tied one onto my line and tried a cast. Kurt didn't fish with me. He was too impatient to sit and flip the hook into the waters where the fish might be, over and over, waiting for their hunger to overtake their caution. A man of direct action, he'd joked that he was the netting sort of fisherman—he'd get in there and scoop out what he wanted.

A second and then a third cast produced nothing. The tip of the rod pointed behind my head as I prepared to cast again, when movement on the other side of the lake drew my eye.

Deer, smaller than the behemoths that had run us down in the smoke, picked their way between the trees. Four animals had come to the water's edge to dip their muzzles into the coolness. It wasn't the season for racks of antlers; all four heads were bare of adornment. One watched while the others drank, then dipped its head to the water. Twilight was their time to feed.

One nibbled on something that sprouted from the bank. I watched, content to let the wild things have the peace of the lake. Then something startled them, and they were gone.

Another cast, and the fly sat on the surface of the water, an enticing morsel to a hungry cutthroat trout. I idly wondered if I really wanted a fish tonight, and had started to reel the fly when something took my hook.

Something big, something feisty and trying to get away. The tip of my rod jerked down, seconds after the fly had disappeared below the surface in the center of expanding ripples. The fish and I dueled from our respective ends of the line. I worked it closer to me, the rod dipping and jinking as the fish fought to escape me. "Come to me, my pretty," I crooned to the fish flapping in the shallows, but when I'd beached the beautiful, fourteen-inch cutthroat, I couldn't bear that it should die by my hand. It had done nothing to deserve a wanton death—I wouldn't eat it tonight.

The hook pierced its lip, so I clipped the barb with my pliers. The hook slipped out, giving me the chore of remounting the fly, but allowing the trout to live without encumbrance. I helped the flapping, struggling fish regain the lake, where it lay in the shallows, sucking great gouts of water through its gills, gathering the strength to disappear. A quick flash and it was gone.

There would be no more casts tonight; I had caught and released my fish. Instead, I would lie back in the grass and watch the sky. The stars were coming out into the indigo of the night, which would fade to black soon. The moon would rise sometime, but for now the pinpoints of the Milky Way were a path through the sky. I looked up, hands behind my head, and tried to recall the names of the brighter stars. Arcturus. Mizer, Merak, Dubhe in the Big Dipper, and Polaris I could find; the others were a bigger mystery. The constellations I knew better: the Big and Little Dippers, Draco, Boötes. The Big Dipper was part of Ursa Major, the Big Bear, and that was as close as I wanted to get to any bear at all, though our visitor from the other day might still be near. I'd like to lie on my back near Kurt, with the breezes soft across our skins, and point out what I knew to him. He might know more—he so often did—and I would watch his finger trace a picture in the stars.

Back to hoping that what Kurt and I had started might continue. I wanted to feel his mouth under mine, I wanted to pull his thighs around me, I wanted… I wanted to have a lot of things with him that I couldn't even imagine properly, so I recalled what we'd done in our frenzy in the cave. Once again I opened my fly and let my rampant cock out to meet my palm. Kurt had touched me, he held me, he slipped his lips over all of my cock, taking it deep into the wet heat of his mouth. My hand rose and fell, slowly this time, as I tried to recapture what had been too fleeting. I could feel him once again tonguing me and imagined his head blocking out the stars, rising and falling over me, sucking and licking. I wanted more of that, I wanted more of him, and this might be the only way I'd get it. My thumb rolled over the head of my cock, spreading the drops I leaked, becoming Kurt's tongue in my mind. The tight, one-fingered grip I switched to became his lips; a little reality helped my imagination along, but I wanted him, not the ersatz and memories.

I wanted… I wanted everything that Kurt could do to me. My utilities got shoved over my lifted butt and down toward my ankles. I lay on my back, letting the breezes whisper through the short hairs as I drew my knees up and apart. Slipping my fingers into my mouth wet them enough to try something new. I brushed them lightly down my chest and belly toward my ass. I had to be ready for him to fuck me, if he would fuck me—no, when he fucked me, I wouldn't let it be any other way now. I would be ready for him. Squeezing my eyes shut, I did what I wanted him to do, touching, probing, preparing. My own hand felt strange; I wanted it to be Kurt who looked down on me and inserted first his fingers and then his cock. I wanted to see his face and feel him stretch me. I wanted to open enough to let him in. Somehow, I would make it all happen—I had to, or it wouldn't happen. Two were too many. I had to back off to one finger—Kurt's finger, at least in my mind. After so much practice imagining his hands, his body, I could imagine he was touching me now. Glorious and yet inadequate—I'd have to do more. Screaming, "Fuck me, Kurt!" into the night helped me feel my hand as his, and then I yelled again as my climax rolled through me. Semen launched toward the stars when the spasms took my breath and left me panting in the grass.

But I lay alone by the water; even the animals had left me. Surely every fish had retreated to the bottom of the lake, and Kurt was miles away.

I refastened my pants and went back to staring at the sky, thinking of Kurt and wondering if he was a better fisherman than he'd let on. In my post-orgasmic haze, the last week looked more and more as if he'd trailed himself like bait before my avid eyes, ever more enticingly, as I stubbornly stayed in the depths, hungry but afraid to lunge. Had the fire provided his net, that he could finally scoop me up for his trophy? The lump in my throat refused to be swallowed down—had he caught me only to throw me back?

TWENTY-THREE

The chugging diesel engine brought me down from the ridge, binoculars in hand. My heart leapt to my throat, and I strained to hear. Was it our truck? Was Kurt coming back? Or had another ranger come to tell me bad news? I couldn't see the road in the slanting evening light.

Yet another day of running back and forth between the lookout point and the archery range had left me able to travel the path without looking down. Good thing, because I was craning my neck for a glimpse of Kurt. Coulda's, shoulda's, woulda's all danced in time with my frantically beating heart.

Missing him and not being quite sure what to say when I saw him left me desperate and confused on top of all my other emotional turmoil. He was always confident, except for that one moment when he thought I didn't want what he offered, so maybe he'd have some idea of how to start the awkward conversation that we were going to have to have. Days of whirling thoughts hadn't brought anything any clearer in my mind about what he might want, though I knew exactly what I wanted.

Kurt. I wanted Kurt, and I could only hope he'd want me

too. Abigail should have said "Don't hurt him" to him instead of me. Maybe she did. I could hope.

The nice thing about sound carrying in the mountains is that I had enough time to find some clean clothes, brush my teeth, and scrape the stubble off my face. Kurt pulled up by the cabin in time to see me come out and wave, which made him wave back and poke his finger at the passenger seat. I swung in beside him. Electricity danced between us, and not a storm cloud in the sky.

"I brought your hat back." Kurt handed it to me like it hadn't been sitting on the seat, waiting. I'd missed it these last few days in the sun, so I put it on. It felt oddly warm. Kurt's own head was bare.

"Thanks," I replied, everything I wanted to say somehow balling up in my chest and refusing to come out. So I said the first damned thing that didn't quite go through my mind, just my nose. "Smells good in here."

"Mrs. Chief sent you a care package. Hungry?" He started to reach behind the seat.

"Uh…." Yes, now, but… "In a bit." My gut contradicted me with a growl, but—not yet. "How's the ankle?"

"Fine, now." Could the small talk get any smaller?

He threw the truck into gear, then headed for the rocky path down to the water.

"I left the tank empty," he explained and wouldn't pull over when I suggested I should thread the narrow track to the water. "I need to be able to do it."

That sounded grim. So did the scrape of branches on the passenger side. Maybe I should take that one tree down, since it seemed to be the biggest obstacle.

Once at the water, he jumped out and unfastened the intake. Kurt's hands on the hose made me think of his hands on me back in the cave—I had to swallow a moan. He glanced up at me and glanced away again before he dropped the intake into the lake while I turned away to start the pump. Guess we were going to have to clear the air right now because we were both so tense we could have twanged.

He looked better than a guy who'd spent days on a fire line had a right to. Mrs. Chief must have taken mercy on him and let him use the washing machines at the house, because I couldn't see him huddled in a towel at the laundromat, watching green clothing spin around.

Moving down the bank to get away from the noise of the pump, we studied each other with wary eyes, two gunslingers waiting for the other to make a move. Kurt drew first. "You look awful. When was the last time you ate or slept?"

I'd been sleeping well once I got into the right bed to do it. Last night I got directly into Kurt's bag, and the crickets sang me to sleep after a while. The other, though—I just shrugged.

Kurt snorted. "Thought so." He marched back to the truck and brought one of the bags. "Here. Eat." He held a chocolate brownie by my mouth as I stared at him. "Come on, eat it."

I wanted to nibble the morsel from his hand, but his gruff manner made me hesitate. "Jake, you can eat it or I can shove it up your nose, but it's going into you. You need it." He pressed it to my lips, and I opened them to take a bite. Chewing and swallowing the mouthwatering chocolate treat activated my brain enough that I took the remaining bite of the brownie from his fingers the same way, instead of reaching up to take it and feed myself. He shuddered and reached into the bag for more food. "Good. I brought you some of Mrs. Chief's fried chicken."

We sat on a fallen tree where he handed me a piece of golden brown deliciousness—even his strained manner couldn't stop me now that I had been made totally aware of my hunger. Another piece disappeared before I thought to ask him if he'd eaten.

"I ate before I left town. No, don't talk to me before you've finished." Kurt handed me a plastic fork and a container of homemade macaroni salad, which got chased down by another drumstick and a bottle of water. I did feel a lot better in one way, but worse in another because I was so scared of what he was going to tell me. He regretted everything, I just knew it, and he'd tell me good-bye after he fed me. The very thought made me feel like I was going to throw up. Waste of good chicken.

"Why did you want me to eat so bad?" I waved away the other brownie he offered.

He put the brownie back into the bag at his feet and stared out over the water before turning to meet my eyes. "I thought that if your blood sugar came up into detectable ranges first that you might not ask me to move out right away."

I goggled at him. "Kurt, that didn't even cross my mind! I wouldn't ask you to leave!" He didn't want to go!

He sighed. "So you've decided to leave instead."

I'd spent the days fearing getting thrown out, but no way in hell would I leave! "No! Kurt…."

He wasn't listening; he was sunk in his own thought. "It's been bothering you, I can tell. You haven't been eating, you haven't been sleeping, you've been thinking about it and going crazy that we did it…."

"Yeah, Kurt, I have been thinking about it a lot, and going crazy, but—"

He interrupted again. "I really did think we were going to buy the farm, and I had to, Jake, I had to ask. I couldn't stay there waiting for the flames without saying something, and you made it so easy. I had to touch you once before…"

"That's what I thought, too, Kurt," I tried to interject, but he talked right over me.

"So now that we're going to live, maybe you can't stand to be around me after that," he concluded miserably.

I rose to my feet, put my hand on his upper arm and dragged him up too. "I can stand it just fine, Kurt."

"You say that, but you've been so disturbed that you haven't been—"

This time I interrupted him in the only way I thought might get his attention and make my point. I kissed him. Completely, thoroughly, and if he didn't like fried-chicken-breath kisses, too bad. My hands on his upper arms kept him from sagging out of reach as I stroked my tongue over his. My mouth over his kept him from uttering any more nonsense. It lasted until I let him up for air.

"Oh, Jake, I've been so freaked out about this. I was so certain you were going to walk out on me after—"

There was more than one way to interrupt his babble. I pushed him in the lake.

He came up sputtering, spewing, and maybe with a clearer head. "What the fuck was that for?" He glared at me as he stroked the few feet to the shore.

I stood with my arms akimbo, watching him heave out of the water. "Maybe now you'll let me get a word in edgewise?"

"Maybe." He removed his boots before taking the hand I offered. "Depends on what you have to say. My boots are soaked."

I swung him to his feet and into my arms for another kiss, which he got before he quite made contact with me. No reason for us both to get wet. "They'll be dry before you need them again."

"Really?" His face lit up, and he looked like the Kurt I remembered instead of the uncertain man with the lowered eyes. "Why's that?"

"Because you're going to be naked for a while. Because I don't want what we did in the cave to be a 'one time only' thing." I'd only spent days fantasizing about what I wanted with him. But…. Uncertainty flared to life, crushing my resolve. "You do want more, right?"

Kurt parted the clouds on my gloomy existence. "Lots more, Jake." Taking his wet shirt off over his head muffled the words, but once it was off, he could see my face.

Removing soggy denim took four hands. Now Kurt stood before me in nothing but his slick skin and a sunny smile.

"Use my shirt for a towel." I started to pull it off, but he reached to grab my hat first. Holding it by the brim, he glanced at the lake and feinted a throw at the water before tossing it into the grass.

"You really hate my hat, don't you?" I had started to leap after my much-maligned headgear but stopped when it landed safely.

"No." He brought me to his mouth for another kiss. "I just like to tease you about it."

I wiped him down, lingering in crevices where water might collect, swiping slowly over the planes of his stomach and back. He reached to my shoulder, saying, "I was scared that only the fear of dying made you say yes."

"That's what bothered me more than anything, Kurt." Kneeling before him to run the shirt down his legs brought me to eye level with his cock, which was slowly recovering from the cold dip in the lake. Rising to about half mast called for a celebratory kiss, which I placed on the firming shaft. An experimental lick to follow the kiss made him gasp, so I tried it again, thinking fast. I'd have a new experience of my own here in about a minute. One more kiss there and I had to stand up because I needed a few more minutes before opening my mouth for him. All of a sudden I knew I could fulfill a fantasy that had been pursuing me since the day I first really noticed him, standing in the shower from the hose. "I was afraid that maybe I was nothing but a new experience, kind of the last opportunity to check off a box before the fire got us."

His hair had dripped down, leaving trickles of water on his neck and shoulders. I put my mouth to his skin to lick up the rivulets, trailing my tongue upward to catch them as they escaped his hair. Kurt tilted his head for me to reach his neck better and moaned softly as I lapped him from collarbone to ear. Holding him close against my bare chest, I felt him warm from the chill of the lake, growing against my groin.

"No, Jake, that wasn't it at all." Catching his earlobe in my teeth cut his words off in a gasp.

"Better tell me what it was, then," I breathed softly against the captured flesh.

"I spent most of two weeks trying to get your attention, and you have to ask that? I did everything but drop one wing and run in circles," he told me in a shaky voice.

"Two weeks?" My assumed indifference had to have been stronger than I knew, but those last few days had gotten my attention all right; he was telling me what I most wanted to hear about those days, and he wasn't throwing me back. I put my hands on his ass to close the distance between us, working my fingers over the muscles there, and it felt better than I had imagined too.

"Yeah, two weeks. I couldn't be really blatant about it, just in case you didn't swing my way, but—true confession, Jake—I wanted you from the start. The moment I put your face to the name on the roster, I thought *Oh shit, I'm in trouble* 'cause you're everything I ever wanted in a man. Aside from being a raging greenhorn in the wilderness, but that was probably fixable."

"That's why you tried to throw me back before orientation even started?" I hadn't forgotten that muttered conversation.

"How the hell was I going to survive a summer with you around?" He came even closer. "But the night we rode into Rifle on my bike, I knew you could get interested."

Oh yeah. I'd managed to rub eight inches of interest against his ass. And I wanted to do it again, right now.

"Best damned sparkplug wire I ever stole." He put his hands down the back of my utilities and played with my butt, too, cupping one cheek with tiny, rhythmic squeezes. "And then I thought we were out of time to be subtle."

"True confession—I wanted you so bad, but I wasn't sure you were sending signals on purpose." I paused to explore a muscle in his neck, which made him moan. "I've been going ber—wait, you *broke my car?*"

"Not exactly. Well, a little. I figured eighty miles on a motorcycle would tell me how careful I'd have to be. And I fixed it."

I just shook my head. "You're something else. But I was going berserk thinking about you." That's all he needed to know —the turmoil was best forgotten entirely.

"You were?" Kurt threw his head back to let me explore some more and rubbed his groin against mine, which reminded me of something I'd planned to do.

"Hell, yes. Haven't jacked off so much since I was a kid and discovered that I could." I wasn't going to mention what I'd been doing yesterday and today that went with it. Let him think I had natural talent.

"That explains the muscular development. You must be ambidextrous." He playfully pinched my biceps.

I made him yelp with a little bite on his shoulder. This was like normal, only with full body contact. I could get to like this kind of teasing a lot. A kiss landed on top of the bite.

"So why did I have to do everything but a pole dance to get your attention?"

"Because I didn't think I could be so lucky as to get a partner who'd be interested in me." I was still having trouble believing it. "Especially after you tried to shed me on eight seconds' acquaintance. You were on 'enforced ignore'." Which gave us a chance to become friends first—I'd be getting sweaty with a man I liked and admired. Love? Check back with me at the end of the fire season.

"You enforced it pretty well. I was beginning to think I misread the situation."

I'd ask him later how else I'd given myself away, but right now I'd rather convince him he was right all along. A handful of buttock, some hip action, and some tongue should be pretty persuasive. Except—

"Hang on a minute." The sound of the pump had changed. I'd have to go turn it off. That meant letting go of Kurt, but then I'd get to return. "Go sit down over there." I shoved him toward the fallen tree with a pat on the ass. "I'll be right back."

TWENTY-FOUR

Heading behind the truck to get the pump switch gave me a minute to decide what to do. I could leave my utility pants and boots over here and stalk back to him naked, or I could drive him mad with anticipation, the good kind, by leaving them on. What I had in mind I could do with pants on, once I moved this throbbing erection into a better position.

Silence fell as the pump stopped, gauge at five hundred gallons. Nothing but mountain sounds—a few bird calls, the croak of a raven, the whisper of the breeze in the trees—accompanied me back to the fallen log where Kurt sat. One leg stretched out in front of him, the other foot back, he leaned back far enough to keep his erection from poking his belly. I'd keep that from being a problem for him.

Forcing myself to go slowly instead of running back to him made me saunter rather than walk. Unplanned but effective, it made his eyes go wide in the late afternoon sun that slanted down on us. Certain at last that he wanted what I wanted, I let my need flood my face. So much pent-up desire made my lips go dry; I licked them for comfort and also because I wanted them moist for what was coming. First a kiss, with my hands on his shoulders, and then I'd travel slowly down the length of his body with my hands, tantalizingly, maddeningly. When I reached his waist, I started to go to my knees. Now, at last, I would repay the glorious things he'd done to me.

Kurt admired my body with yearning as naked as my own before wrapping his arms around my shoulders. "You're sure you want to do this?" he asked me before placing his lips to mine.

"Never surer." My hands roamed over his groin. I'd had days to decide, and I wanted this above all else: to touch him and be touched by him, in every way.

I could kiss him as I explored, gently, taking the time to feel his textures. Crisp, curly hairs against my fingertips, soft skin over hard shaft, thicker skin covering his balls, perfect for cupping. I played him with both hands, slowly this time, wanting him to feel everything I could imagine doing. I had daylight; I could look too, but that meant taking my mouth from his, something I wasn't willing to do just yet.

One hand under his sack, the other on his shaft, I stroked my thumb over the head of his cock in perfect time with the stroke of my tongue, feeling the slickness in both places. Kurt moaned, and that was my signal to do something that would bring louder noises. I needed to hear my name rumble from his throat, erupting from someplace deeper within. He'd done it for me—now I'd do it for him.

Taking the time to look let me admire his hard cock, full and thick. Smaller than my own but still more than a handful and a mouthful, he had to be right about seven inches long, and thick. I'd worry about what that meant for other things later; now I wanted to put my mouth over the glistening head and flick the little slit with my tongue. From my place between his knees, I could do that.

Kurt's hands were flat on my back, gently encouraging me to bend to him, to take his rigid length with my mouth for the very first time. My name was a whisper with the wind as he breathed it out, his scent a combination of salt and musk as I breathed it in. So soft and still firm, so smooth. I licked the head and its salty droplets, before venturing farther down to lick along his shaft. My lips rubbed his length with each movement of my head, tongue flicking along from base to tip. Slowly, then faster, then slowly again, coming back to where prickly hairs tickled my cheek before rising up and capturing him with my mouth completely. Down I went, taking as much of him in as I could, and up again to end with the lightest of tickles before sucking him back in. If my imagination hadn't been equal to the reality of him sucking me, neither had it been equal to the reality of me sucking him. I could make him feel as good as he'd done me and enjoy the sensuous feel of him against my tongue, his hands in my hair.

With every stroke and his every small moan, I gained confidence, sucking him more deeply into my mouth. Until I found my gag reflex with the head of his cock. But he only stroked my shoulders until I finished choking and sputtering. Okay, this was a skill—and Kurt would be as good a teacher for this as for archery. I bent again to engulf him.

Kurt moaned my name, but I wanted to hear more. I wanted him to explode, calling my name. I'd put my hands on his waist for balance, but now I needed one for his solid shaft, wet with my saliva and throbbing against my palm. The little veins jumped under my fingertips as I caught a breath, licking the edge of the head because I couldn't bear to take my mouth away, and then I plunged down on him, stopped only by my hand, which rose against my lips with each stroke.

"Not going to last long," he choked out, his hands tight on my shoulders now.

"Good," I took a moment to say, my hand never stopping, before resuming the downward trek with my lips. I meant it, too. I wanted him to come in my mouth, I wanted to taste him, I wanted to know that he climaxed because of how good I made him feel. It would mean that I was doing it right even though I'd never done it before, which I hoped he couldn't tell. If I was messing it up, maybe he'd teach me better, but it suddenly didn't seem to be a problem.

Kurt's climax rippled through him an instant before come spurted out into my mouth, followed by his shout of pleasure. If it wasn't my name, that was okay, because he started saying "Oh, Jake, oh, Jake…" a moment later, before I'd quite made up my mind to swallow the thick, salty proof of his orgasm. In order to respond to him I'd have to do something, and a moment later only a slightly bitter aftertaste remained.

Rocking back onto my heels let me make enough lap for Kurt to straddle me. I had to feel as much of his skin as I could. He wrapped his arms around me, still murmuring my name. I held him tightly, my face pressed against his chest, while I caught my breath and he caught his. It also put his groin right against mine, which made my hips move almost involuntarily against him. Even through the britches, it was enough to tip me over after what I'd been doing to him. I moaned into his skin with my climax, the waves of pleasure amplified by the man I held.

"Crikey!" I mumbled. I hadn't even gotten my pants off.

"I knew you'd say it eventually," Kurt reassured me through his laughter. "The beauty of being a twenty-two-year-old horndoggy is that you'll be ready to go again in no time." Yeah, with Kurt in my arms, I would be ready again fast. "It also gives us a few minutes to get some other things done." He looked down into my eyes before he kissed me and got to his feet. I liked what I saw in their sky-blue depths. I let him pull me up, too, and held him tightly before peeling down to rinse my underwear in the lake. I recalled the "commando" incident. Had that really happened less than two weeks ago? Seemed like years now.

"Naked together at last," Kurt observed, eyes dancing. It was kind of funny—four orgasms and no nudity until afterward, and I realized I was laughing for the first time since we left the cave with Max. For that I had to hug him again.

"Come on," Kurt said, "let's get up to the cabin while we still have some light." He led me to the truck, where we threw our clothes into the cab.

Something crackled from behind the seat. I extracted a brown paper bag and peeked in. "What's this?" I pulled out a large blue carton, the sort that meant he had hit the warehouse store in Gypsum.

"Hope in a box," he told me, with eyes that didn't dance quite so much. "There's lube too."

"And a lot of it." I pulled a warehouse-store-sized bottle out of the bag to go with the condoms. "Kurt, you had to have some faith that I wouldn't throw you out or you wouldn't have bought all this."

"No, just a lot of hope." He started up the engine. "I had visions of blowing them all up like balloons for the foxes to play with if you left."

Forty balloons would keep the foxes entertained for a while. And probably raise a few hikers' eyebrows. "You do realize that this will only last a month, don't you?" I grinned at his expression, a combination of anticipation and shock, glad to have shaken the grimness that had threatened to come back. Flabbergasted beat sad.

"You are a horndoggy, aren't you?" he asked lightly. He pulled up the rocky road to the cabin. Making that truck go forward wasn't a problem.

I pondered that accusation and decided that not only was it a good thing but that I wasn't the only one in this truck. He pulled up next to my Toyota. "So are you. The giant economy box is a good idea. I do believe—" Instead of getting out, I stopped to make him look at me. "—that we are going to need every single one."

TWENTY-FIVE

Same porch, same crooked shutter, same stone chimney. The cabin appeared exactly as I'd left it but somehow felt different, I thought, as Kurt and I carried bags in from the truck. He was here, he was happy to be here with me, and that turned our sixteen-by-sixteen hut into home again.

We could find places on the shelves for our new toys once we were done playing, but could we play on the cots without collapsing a leg or two? I eyed them with the sort of longing that should have made them *sproing* into a California king mattress with a pillowtop, but they stubbornly remained thirty-inch-wide Army surplus canvas with our sleeping bags draped haphazardly over the narrow frames. "Think we should drag the cots together?"

"There'll be a ridge in the middle and it will be tippy." He flapped his rumpled bag open. "I thought I left this thing straight."

Suddenly, he turned to me, dawning realization on his face. "I did leave it straight. You never do." He began to laugh softly. "If I'd come into the cabin before I talked to you, I would've known. I could have saved myself all that anguish and a dip in the lake."

My face heated—I tried to laugh it away. "It was the only way I could get any sleep at all."

"I intend to wear you out enough that you'll sleep like a log tonight," he told me with a grin, so I pulled him close and kissed him. "Now, fold up that miserable excuse for a sleeping surface. Condoms weren't the only thing I bought in Gypsum."

"Oh?" I followed Kurt out to the truck, where he opened an equipment hatch, revealing a queen-sized air mattress in a box.

"Are you sure it wasn't faith in me sticking around that sent you shopping?" I asked again as we unfolded blue vinyl on the floor. "And where's the pump?"

"'Charge for one hour before use'," Kurt read, and we looked sourly at the grapefruit-sized air pump that would do us no good at all right this minute.

"We can plug it into the truck," I consoled him.

"By the time we blow the mattress up ourselves the damned pump will be charged." He seethed, and I couldn't blame him—I wanted him and comfort, and I wanted them *now*, without a side of hyperventilation.

"I have another idea." I took him into my arms. "I'd really rather be outside, down by the lake. Wouldn't you?"

"Yes. I wasn't thinking," Kurt replied, rubbing his hand up and down my back. "Or I was, but only about sleeping next to you for the rest of the season."

"Good thought, but for tonight...." I waved my brows wickedly. "Hey, I have to go retrieve the archery equipment before it gets full dark. Meet you there at the lake?"

My last sight of him was bare legs in boots poking out from beneath a moving mound of sleeping bags as he headed down the path to the water.

Something about running around in the woods in near dark while naked didn't appeal, so I yanked my utilities and boots back on for the hike back to the archery range. The possums I didn't want for pets would be quick to gnaw the bow's salt-laden handgrip. I wouldn't leave the bow and arrows out overnight to be chewed on by them or the skunks, porcupines, and raccoons that all craved the salt.

With the quiver at my waist and the unstrung bow across my shoulder, I trotted over to the target to pull the arrows out. This time, they were all in one ring or another, and one protruded from the very edge of the gold center circle. Kurt would be pleased with my hard work over the last few days, I thought. I gave a quick pat to the aspen tree that had been such a pal to both of us, feeling a little foolish. Then I headed back to the cabin, confident that the night could only continue to be good.

The sky had shaded to purple and aqua at the edges by the time I returned to the lake. Kurt had zipped the two opened bags together at the end and arranged himself picturesquely across the blue rip-stop nylon. He smiled up at me, his hand out to welcome me to our bed. "I get to undress you at last?"

"Oh, yeah!" He'd chosen a spot on the grassy edge of the lake, near a stand of fir trees. Not too near the water, I noticed with a chuckle. Didn't want to toss my boots in by accident, so I left them several steps away in the grass.

I breathed in the fresh mountain air, scented with grasses and pine, thinking there was no other place on earth I'd rather be, and no one else I'd rather share it with. A perfect evening, one of many I hoped to have before summer gave way to fall.

Kurt was completely bare except for the shadows painted on him by the fading light. The moon would rise later, but for now, he was mysteriously vague in his nakedness. I'd touch him all over, didn't need light for that. Kneeling next to him let him put his hands at my fly, where I'd had my own so often, but not tonight. He unzipped me slowly, running his hands over my groin, making me shiver. His hands traveled over more of me, up my chest and around my waist as he kissed my chest, licking me now and then. I ran my hands over him, too, wanting him to hurry and slip my clothing off, yet wanting to stretch out the moment.

Warm fingers finally crept under my briefs. Kurt ran his hands down my thighs as he took my britches down. The evening breeze tickled me when the fabric came away—once again he was right, I'd recovered fast. Didn't think he was very far behind me, either, though I couldn't see and he wasn't plastered against me. He would be soon. Now, in fact, because he pushed me down onto the open sleeping bag to strip the utilities away. Once I was bare, Kurt stretched out on top of me, mouth to mine, body to mine, skin to skin. He was hard—I could feel him pressed against my belly next to my own erection. I wanted to lose myself in his kiss, so I closed my eyes and let our tongues explore.

My hand went exploring, too—I checked every inch I could reach, from the muscles in his back to the round globes of his butt. I squeezed, I stroked, I grabbed, all to take in the feeling of him. He'd stressed the importance of learning the terrain. I assumed that was true for the terrain of his body as much as the land. I thought I'd be a better student for Kurt's own landscape.

"Tell me what you want," he invited between kisses. "Tell me what you like."

I froze. "I don't know." I'd been dreading explaining—it was just one more area where Kurt had experience and I did not.

"If you don't know, who does?" He cocked his head slightly, then closed his eyes slowly. He figured it out fast about the sleeping bags, and he deciphered this, too, in record time. I could practically hear gears turning in his head, which was good because I didn't want to say the words.

He leaned to whisper in my ear. "Oh, Jake…. What have you done before?" I didn't think he was supposed to ask that, but what else was he going to say? The slow motion of his hips stopped, but his arms tightened around me.

The heat had to be rising off my face detectably. "Uh, a little oral."

"When? Just this week?" At least he was asking questions in the least embarrassing way possible.

"Yeah. That's all." I lay back and shut my eyes tight. "Well, some touching before."

"That's okay, Jake," Kurt told me, stroking my face with his cheek. "It makes sense of some other stuff. I'm glad you told me." He kissed me again, a barely perceptible brush of lips against mine. "I'm glad you trust me enough to tell me. If there's something you don't even want to try, we won't."

"I want to try it all!" I said fiercely, rolling him over so that I lay on top of him. "Everything!" I remembered my doubts about being able to fit inside him. "Everything that you're okay with."

"I'm okay with trying everything too." Kurt gazed deeply into my eyes, connecting us with a hot flare of unspoken passion before connecting us physically with more open-mouthed kisses.

Then we tried kisses everywhere—necks, shoulders, chests—and hands everywhere, as we rolled over. His skin tasted salty, and he smelled of musk and masculinity. His muscular body felt so right plastered to mine. The evidence of his arousal rubbed my hip, and I suddenly had to use my tongue there, too, so I flipped around. I did this earlier for him, which he liked a lot, so if I tried it again, I'd be starting from solid ground. From between his thighs, I could suck him long and slow.

I took him into my mouth and let my tongue work over the head of his cock. We had time to try everything now, so I did: with lips, with tongue, with my hand. Some things made him cry out—I took careful note of those—other things made him sigh, and his hand was gentle as he ran fingers through my hair. He leaned up on one elbow to watch me, making me wish for the moon to come up so I could better see his face. The starlight wasn't bright enough yet, though it was getting a bit brighter.

Behind his head, the aqua faded to azure, a spattering of bright pinpricks adorning the heavens. God, how beautiful, and more so to be enjoying it with Kurt. I closed my eyes against the loveliness, focusing on my task.

"You need some too," he told me after I spent a long time trying to drive him crazy, and suddenly he was straddling my head and leaning over me. That put his cock where I could reach again. He took my cock in one hand and then his mouth. "Turnabout and all that," he came up long enough to say before he started slowly destroying my sanity with his tongue.

Writhing and whimpering was about all I could manage. I couldn't do him justice with what he was doing to me, so I had to let his cock slip from my mouth. I could kiss and nibble his inner thighs without worry as he played me, and when he came up for air, I took him again with my lips. One hand for his cock, one hand for his ass, and then he drove thoughts away with his mouth on me again.

If this continued much longer, I'd come again. It would be wonderful, but it would mean waiting on some of the other things I thought we both wanted. With his ass over me like that, I could see the dark crevasse between his cheeks where I'd been yearning to explore.

"Whoa there, Kurt." I ran a hand under his chest to raise him. "Got to let me be for a bit." I kissed his balls for a consolation before he turned around to drop against my side.

"I got more yelling out of you in the cave," he said with a smile, barely visible in the waning light. "Wasn't I doing it right?"

"More than right, and you know it." I slapped his ass affectionately, the sound sharp against the night noises of the mountain. "I had something to muffle on this time."

"Muffling, huh. New name for it. You about made me come. Were you planning to?" He gave me an arm for a pillow and bent his head to mine while we both pulled back from the brink.

"I plan to do that a lot, only thought we'd try another thing or two first," I told him. I ran a hand over his hip. I felt like a kid in a candy store, so much try, but what to choose first?

"Mmmm, such as?"

I'd thought about it on the way back from the archery range. I thought I was ready. The words weren't coming easily though. I had to nibble his ear before I could say, "I want you to do me." For some reason I couldn't quite meet his eyes.

He moaned at the words. "I've been wanting that for so long. Just, don't let's make it have to be all tonight, if you aren't feeling ready when...."

"I'll be ready. We'll be great." I pulled him on top of me again and let my hips pump a tiny bit against him. I faked an easy smile, hoping he wouldn't feel how badly I trembled.

"We'll try getting you ready, but Jake, we have all the time in the world. You don't have to push it if...." I could hear the anticipation in his voice right there with the hesitation. He wanted it as badly as I did, but not enough to hurt me. Then again, I wouldn't be so trusting if I hadn't known he'd be considerate.

I feigned a nonchalance I didn't truly feel. "You aren't the only one with high hopes, Kurt. I'm ready." I pushed my forehead and nose against his to speak at closest range. A Cyclops stared back, surprise in his one bright eye. "Or I will be, once you play with me a while."

"Do I even want to know the source of this optimism?" he asked but wisely didn't wait for an answer he wasn't going to get. Instead, he rolled us over so he could reach the bottle of lube. "Hang on to this," he said after he poured some over his hand and rubbed his fingers.

I had tried hard to make up my mind which I wanted more, to do him first or for him to do me. I was less likely to mess up if I let him show me the way, I decided—not without trepidation now that I'd handled him. Still, when he knelt between my knees, that was the place I wanted him to be most of all. He reached for my ass.

"Okay, just relax, Jake," he whispered hoarsely, as he touched me and slipped one fingertip inside. That felt so much better than my own finger—I whooshed out a breath. On my next inhalation his finger slid in further.

It had to be a rush for him to do that, every bit as much as it was for me. Low, needy sounds rumbled out of my chest as he slipped in and out, expanding me, preparing me, fucking me with his finger. "You're too damned far away" brought him kneeling over me, close enough to touch, close enough to kiss, but never stopping the slow, persistent action. It was good, and it got better because he never stopped kissing me as he penetrated me with gentle fingers, adding as he felt I could take them. Once, I asked him to pause, but a moment's rest and some more lube and I was ready for him to go on.

"Come where I can reach you" made him knee-walk to my side. I used two hands to put the condom on him, then the lube to slick him. Kurt moaned when I did it. The moon peeked over the treetops, so I could finally see his face. So much yearning showed, all for me. The pure intensity of it took my breath away. "I'm ready, Kurt."

"How do you want me?" he rasped, still moving his fingers slowly into me.

"I need to see your face" was all I could tell him, and hoped he'd know what to do with that. He did—he climbed between my knees again, bringing his shaft close to my ass.

"You're sure?" I could tell it cost him to hesitate, but he didn't ask again when I whispered my yes. With my legs wrapped around him for leverage, he used his hand to guide himself, and then he pushed his hips forward.

TWENTY-SIX

Kurt lay panting on top of me. He might have caught his breath more easily if I hadn't been squeezing him so tightly. I forced my arms to relax slightly, and I made up for it by running one hand up and down his back, feeling gooseflesh on his skin. He exhaled with an "Ahhh," and lay more heavily against me.

He was a welcome weight, a welcome presence in my body. He'd finally entered me, his cock sliding inside me with some slippery effort, filling me, stretching me. He went slowly at first, letting me get used to his cock inside. Leaning over for kisses let me see his face. The faint glow from the quarter moon glistened in his eyes, wide with wonder. Kurt's mouth changed with his movements: now a smile, then lips parted with pleasure, later scrunched together in a hard line of concentration. Mine had to be doing the same because happiness ran together with sensation.

"Relax, Jake. Don't fight me. That'll make it hurt."

The stretching bordered on pain, but I breathed through my mouth, willing my body to let him in. His fingers brushing lightly over my sides helped me let go of the stress that urged me to clamp down and fight the intruder.

If imagination hadn't come close to the reality of Kurt's mouth, neither had my practice alone come close to the reality of Kurt inside me. He stroked slowly, pushing in and slipping out, gaining speed as I encouraged him with sounds, hands, and legs. The pain receded, leaving pleasure in its wake. I rested my heels on his shoulders, making the happy discovery that he could lean on my thighs and I could direct him without words.

Words beyond "Kurt!" and "Oh!" and "Ah!" were neither needed nor possible as he rocked his hips against my butt. Now and then he'd ask, "Like this?" and I'd nod or moan, amazed at what he could do to me. I was totally vulnerable to him, and he used it to bring me joy.

Not that I was just lying back, enjoying—I had to touch him, too. Holding his upper arms to brace him gave way to sliding my hands all over his shoulders and sides, where the hard ridges of muscle moved. Once, he reared up away from my thighs, letting me stroke his chest. Finding the hard nubs of his nipples solved a mystery; he liked them played with every way I found to do it, judging from the noises he made. I was making plenty of noises of my own, especially when he pressed against something inside that felt wonderful.

Kurt had reached for my cock, intending to pump me as he fucked me, but I stopped him with a small shake of my head and a quick hand—we'd save that for later. What we were doing now needed my complete attention, and my brain was shutting down to the narrow awareness that the man I yearned for was giving me everything I'd dreamed of and more. I wanted it to last forever, I wanted him to explode with climactic pleasure. I wanted it all and at the same time.

Kurt blocked out the sky as I gazed up at him. He lifted

himself to his knees again to be framed by stars, painted with moonlight. I held out my hands; he took them as he changed rhythm. Long, slow strokes gave way to shorter, choppier thrusts as his climax built. His face changed as he pushed inside me.

I'd wanted to see the emotions play across his face at this moment when all his pleasure erupted into me, because of me, for me. His last thrust brought him completely inside me, where he stayed, pulsing and shuddering. I gripped his hands as tightly as I could—he clenched back as the spasms swept through him, shockwave after shockwave of ecstasy. His wordless cry trailed off, his hands opened, and the shuddering became swaying. He collapsed slowly against me, and I took hold of his shoulders to bring him down against my chest.

Now he rested his weight on top of me, panting, his hands slipping under my back, his face in my neck. His breathing mingled with the other mountain sounds: a night bird's cry, a splash in the water as a fish rose. The chorus of frogs and crickets that provided our nightly serenade became something I could hear again, but it faded away when he whispered, "Oh, Jake...."

TWENTY-SEVEN

Kurt rolled us to our sides. "Good?" Like he had to ask.

"Wonderful," I told him as I rubbed his face with my own. The sweat from his exertions made my nose slide across his. "The best. Let's do it again." I wanted him to know exactly how much I wasn't planning to leave, now that we'd completed this new joining.

"Horny boy," he said with a chuckle. "You need to come sometime tonight."

"I plan to," but I wasn't entirely sure how, because he'd filled me enough that I was scared again of hurting him if we switched places.

I think he heard the doubt in my voice. "Something's worrying you," Kurt murmured, with one thumb stroking my cheek. "Tell me."

"Kurt, it's… well, you've seen me. You've held me and all. I'm big." I stopped to think of what to say next. "Buttholes are small. I don't want to hurt you."

"Buttholes are stretchy. You won't." He sounded confident, and I wanted to believe him. "Did I hurt you?"

"I'm feeling it, but no, you didn't." I couldn't leave it alone. "I'm just worried."

"Don't be," he said, looking up to me now and seeing that reassurances weren't working. "True confession, Jake. I had two nights alone in a pup tent on the Chiefs' back lawn after I saw you. Touched you. You won't hurt me." He lay back down with his head on my shoulder now, one leg thrown across my hips. Okay, I could guess—I'd done the same. I supposed the old adage held true about great minds thinking alike.

"For a guy who says he didn't expect me to stick around, you've done a lot of stuff that says otherwise." And I was glad of it, too. "Why were you so afraid, Kurt?" If I did or said something beyond the screw-up I knew about, I wanted to know. "I was jumpy around Carlene. Was it more than that?" He was hurt when I'd pulled away, but I still didn't understand how to respond to that sort of teasing. Maybe if I was further out of the closet, I'd know.

"You reacting like you'd been burned really hurt. It reminded me a whole lot of another time." His breath tickled my chest. "It... happened to me once. Getting dumped hard after a disaster. Halfway up El Capitan. I told you part of the story, not all of it. We were cold and frightened—it was a long way down and a real narrow ledge—and we comforted one another. Next day, the weather cleared, but we climbed down, not up, because he said he didn't trust me any longer. He hasn't spoken to me since."

Oh shit! No wonder his voice wavered when he'd told that story. While my initial reaction bordered on jealousy at the nameless guy who spent time with Kurt, white hot anger trailed right behind. I'd never trusted anyone like I trusted Kurt, and to have someone deliver such a cruel blow...! No wonder he nearly freaked out. I marveled that he even had the nerve to approach me at all, under the circumstances.

My heart broke for him, because this was exactly what I'd been afraid would happen between us. Again, like minds. I was willing to bet that the guy's bitching about meat breath had nothing to do with any salami, either. "He's an idiot, Kurt. There isn't anyone I'd rather have with me in a tough situation, and if he couldn't let the sex part go, or keep you forever, he was a complete idiot." I squeezed him hard, hoping he knew that I'd never let him go so easily. "I'm not going anywhere."

"Good." He squeezed me back.

"This happened about two years ago?" Abigail's words about a broken heart came back to me.

"Just about. How did you know?"

"Because you left civilization behind right about then."

"I like the outdoors." Kurt shrugged with one shoulder. Then he whispered, "Yeah."

Something niggled at the back of my mind. "Kurt, you could probably have climbed the scarp, couldn't you?" The scarp wasn't nearly as high or as vertical as El Capitan.

"Maybe. The ankle would have been one hell of a handicap." He drew lines on my chest with his fingertips, and sounded like he didn't want to pursue it.

I kept on. "Then why didn't you suggest it?"

"Because you couldn't. Or maybe you could, but not without equipment we didn't have. I wasn't going to leave you, okay?" He sounded fierce now, like the admission was getting dragged out of him with hot pincers.

Hot damn, it wasn't just sex for him any more than it was for me. I'd stop pushing now. Start kissing though.

"You didn't leave me when Motorcycle Boy showed up."

Damn it, every time I left his mouth unoccupied, he'd start spouting nonsense again. About stuff I didn't want to discuss.

"'Course not." I kissed him some more and started stroking his neck and shoulders. That ought to have distracted him, but it didn't, because my bowstring-roughened fingers caught his skin. He brought my hand up to his eyes but was defeated by the dim light. Rubbing his thumb over my fingertips told him more, and then he sucked my fingers into his mouth. His tongue explored the forming calluses, soothing and arousing me at the same time, making me moan. I needed a better way to deflect him, because he was asking more questions now.

"You've been at the archery range a lot these last few days?" Then he sucked my fingers back in.

I took my hand away because his mouth was making me lose my caution on this topic.

"Yes." Rolling on top of him might change the subject, besides being exactly what I wanted. I stuck my hip between his thighs and wiggled closer, trying to change the subject.

"Why?"

Tenacity could be a good quality or a bad quality, depending. He simply wouldn't give up.

Telling him to shut up didn't seem appropriate at the moment, and pushing him into the lake wasn't an option. "Improving my aim, Kurt. Why else?" If I got the condom on and got lubed up, we'd see how good my aim was at short range. I started groping after the foil packet that had to be somewhere close by.

"Your aim was pretty damned good when it counted." Kurt handed over the condom.

Ripping the packet open with my teeth bought me a moment. "No, it wasn't, and I wish everyone would stop talking about it like it was." This line of talk was causing my erection to subside. Rubbing against Kurt might help, but I was getting upset, because the Chief, the sheriff, and now Kurt had all praised me when I didn't deserve it.

"Stop." Kurt took the condom out of my hand. Shit—he'd changed his mind! "Don't ever open a rubber like that. They can rip. Geez, Jake, if I didn't know you were a virgin before, I'd know now. Here." He hunted around to the side for another, which he tore open himself. "You were saying?" He tried to unroll it over me, but I wasn't even close to firm enough, even with the relief that he wasn't bringing this dream to a halt.

"Kurt, wait." Okay, I'd tell him. Then he could laugh about something that wasn't my deep desire for him. "My aim that day sucked." I kind of collapsed on top of him, and he held me close, not saying anything, at last. My forehead touched the sleeping bag next to his face as he rubbed my back. "It worked out okay, but that was good luck and not good planning."

"It worked," he pointed out between nibbles at my earlobe.

"Yeah, but I couldn't have deliberately shot that damned bike if your life depended on it, and I thought it did. But you were to my left, and I always—well, not so much now—but I was shooting with a bad left deviation, and I couldn't risk shooting you. So I overcorrected. Shot behind him." I lifted my head to look at him while I confessed this. "Kurt, I was trying to kill him."

My head shadowed his face, because the moon had changed position in the sky, though I could still see his eyes, wide now with understanding. "You were trying to kill him," he echoed, murmured words barely registering.

"He was threatening you." That said everything to me, and it must have said everything to Kurt, because he clutched me tightly and kissed me with a ferocity unlike his previous passion. Even now, days later, I wanted to wipe out the danger and the memory of danger.

"You shouldn't have that on your conscience because of me," he gasped out eventually. "I'm glad you didn't."

"Me, too, but I can't depend on that kind of luck. I have to be able to hit what I'm aiming at." I reached to stroke his cheek, letting him suck my fingers back into his mouth and then release them to speak.

"We'll work on it together," he promised with more licks, and now I might be able to concentrate on what he was saying instead of on him, at least on the range. "The rewards for good shooting will be worth it." Anticipating those rewards might screw up my concentration, but I intended to collect somehow. He grew solemn again. "I have one more thing to tell you, since we're confessing all tonight."

That sounded really bad. I pulled back to better see him, heart pounding.

"When we went into town, you really did bring clean underwear. I hid them." His teeth flashed in the moonlight.

"You what?" My yell silenced Kurt and the night creatures for a few seconds.

"I wanted you to be really, really aware." Kurt laughed, and I did, too, a little, but damn, he had to know what it was like to walk around commando.

He was pinned under me—revenge was mine. "I was, you wretch!" Swift pokes under his arms made him yelp and writhe, but I'd gotten my fingers into his armpits and was merciless. He twisted around enough that he could roll away as I pounced after him, grabbing one foot, but he escaped. While I scrambled to my feet, he danced farther down the shore, laughing and teasing me.

"I stuck them under the front seat of the car. You were six inches away from them all that time! They're still there!"

"Why, you…!" I lunged after him. He stepped back, but caught his heel on a tree root and started to topple backward, which would have sent him for another frigid dip into the lake. He windmilled his arms frantically in an attempt to regain his balance. I managed to catch a wrist as it whirled by and yank him back upright. Since that just happened to throw him against my chest, I could wrap my arms around him and hug him tight. My prisoner showed no inclination to escape. Instead, he put his own arms around me and hugged back. Our mouths met and my eyes closed—a moment later I had to shift him to let my cock stand up between us. Plastered against me once again, Kurt rubbed his belly tantalizingly against me, pulling moans from deep in my throat.

One handful of his ass wasn't enough. I had to reach down and grab his other buttock. Muscles moved under his skin as I pulled him to me, helping him rub. I knew what lay between those flexing cheeks, oh I wanted to turn him, to touch, to be there. Suddenly I couldn't get enough air, and then he took my breath away even more.

"Do me," he whispered into my mouth. "I want you to do me."

Anticipation turned the short steps back to the opened sleeping bags into slow motion. Kneeling down together took an instant and an eternity. Kurt's eyes were nearly closed and his lips were parted. He stroked my body, running warm hands down my chest and belly, catching my cock. Chills followed behind the whispery touch. Two hands made a warm haven for me; he held my shaft as I thrust in tiny, experimental motions. If I leaned on his shoulder, I could reach the abandoned condom, which was still furled. He unrolled it over me, the delayed pleasure just as fine for waiting until we'd cleared the air. Still on our knees while he found the bottle of lube so he could smear some on my cock, he then made sure I was very, very slick, so slick that I had to stop him before I came.

"Let's grease you, too," I murmured, still concerned about hurting him. When he went to his hands and knees before me, I poured lube down his crack and massaged him, reveling in the soft skin, the little ridges, the opening I'd dreamed of breaching. What he'd said about stretching was true, I learned. Kneeling beside him, I slicked him with a finger, my other arm wrapped around him from below, my face against his back. He rocked against my hand, small sounds escaping him, followed by larger sounds, then by choked requests for "More. More."

I gave him more, until the only more I had to give was me. "Get behind me," Kurt whispered. "Come in."

The faint moonlight came from behind us, putting his face into my shadow. "I need to see you."

Kurt rolled to his back, legs open to me, but I'd been there, pinned in one place. "You need to be able to move more than that—you have to be in control here."

He flipped up to his knees to face me. "You are going to drive me crazy, Jake," he said before he kissed me and pushed me down to my back on the sleeping bag.

"Trying to," I suggested, but now I was the one going crazy, because he'd straddled me, sitting in front of my cock. He flexed his hips against me, rubbing me, then rose up enough to point me. The head of my cock was poised at his entrance, then in. We both cried out as he slid down, rocking to bring more of me within him at every move. Slowly he took me in, until he sat against my groin with his full weight, and I could have come just from the tightness of his ass. Kurt panted, sending waves through his torso. I took tiny breaths, trying not to move. We stayed still, getting used to the feel of each other's bodies, until I thought I could risk moving.

With tiny strokes, I shifted my hips, slipping inside him. Kurt helped me by lifting himself and coming back down to my slow rhythm. My hands on his waist guided him, and though he could choose any speed or depth he wanted, he let me set the pace this first time. I could see his face, just as I wanted to, needed to. The moonlight showed me his white teeth between parted lips, as what I did made him turn up to the stars. Tall pines behind us whispered in a light breeze that didn't touch the ground; their needles rustled together and their trunks creaked as they reached to the sky. Kurt's gasps and small cries mixed with the night's sounds.

I wanted Kurt to have control here, but he wanted me to have it, and he made no move unless I moved, or moved him. Up and down, in small strokes, then larger strokes, but not wildly, because wildness would make me come. This had to last, this first wonderful time, as long as I could make it last—for him, for me, for *us*. We might do this again ten thousand times, but never again would it be our first, my first. I pushed up from the sleeping bag, thrusting into his ass, peering into his face, so open, so aroused. He cried out wordlessly as I lifted myself into him again, meeting me midstroke, pulling up and coming down to me.

We drove against each other, one stroke followed by another that brought me ever closer to ending it. I writhed into him, clasped tightly in his ass and his hands. Kurt gripped my arms for leverage, meeting me movement for movement, gasp for gasp.

With my hands on his hips, I dragged Kurt down onto my hard cock—I couldn't bear to let him up again. Deep within him I spurted, pulsing and crying out—it might have been his name that left my throat raw and my heart pounding.

He leaned down to hold me in the aftermath of my orgasm. I curled against his chest, wanting every inch of skin to touch, and he held me tight with one arm, nuzzling me for a moment before gently unhitching himself to drop next to me on the sleeping bag. I groaned as my spent cock slipped out of him. The fires he'd roused in me had flared and banked, but he'd stir them to open flame again soon. Kurt stretched out close to me, propped on one elbow to make his forearm my pillow. His skin was warm where he pressed mine, and the flannel sleeping bag, smelling of shaving cream and his skin, was warm below me. My breath returned after a bit, and I pulled away from his chest enough to look at him.

Sufficient moonlight lit our little nest for me to see his face as he smiled down on me. His dimple, which only showed when he was happy, formed a dark smudge near the right corner of his mouth. I'd had to fight not to touch that dimple only days before. My left hand came up to cup his face, and he leaned into the caress. Kurt, my friend, my companion, was now Kurt, my lover. I didn't have to be afraid to reach for him. Softly, gently, I pressed my thumb into his dimple.

EPILOGUE

We left one can of peas as a joke, and a can of peaches for luck when we cleaned out the bear box for the last time. Fire season was over, the first snows had come, and we hadn't made love by the lake for the last month.

Instead, Kurt would build a fire inside our little cabin, and we'd pull our camp cots in front of the hearth. The air mattress had proven irresistible to the critters that nibbled holes faster than we could patch them, so we were back to Army surplus comfort. Zipping the sleeping bags together had solved everything but the ridge in the middle, but I could reach over from my cot to touch him in the night. Better than any fire, Kurt was my source of warmth.

"Sad to be leaving?" he asked when he found me leaning against the Toyota's open door instead of climbing in. Everything we planned to take was already loaded, and the tanker idled, warming up. We'd return the truck to the Forest Service lot in Meeker to be serviced and put up until next season. Kurt and I had spent some very good hours in that tanker.

"Not sad enough to stay tonight. There's a storm rolling in."

I could read the sky now, but the weather service had five to ten inches of snow forecast. I hugged him hard enough to feel his firm body through his light parka. "But it's been home."

"Home is where you are, Jake," Kurt told me, and met my mouth with his own. Our kiss was good-bye to the cabin, the lake, and the archery range, but not to each other. We had a real apartment waiting for us a hundred miles away. Heat, hot water, a refrigerator, the works.

A double bed, too. We'd laid each other down on picnic tables, fallen logs, and boulders, but an innerspring mattress would be a new experience.

"Where you are too." I could not imagine being without Kurt, my outdoorsy, capable lover, who razzed me, loved me, and made sure life was ever full. "This is the first October in eighteen years that my butt hasn't been in a classroom. That's a little weird."

"Next year," he reminded me. "Enjoy it, but not so much you forget to show up for pharmacy school." He kissed me again and pinched my ass. "Let's get rid of that noisy truck."

Kurt aimed the tanker down our dirt track toward town; I followed him in the car. I would follow him to Wapiti Creek, a posh ski resort deep in the Colorado Rockies, where we'd paint hotel rooms and wait for the lifts to open. I'd find some seasonal job, and Kurt thought he'd teach skiing or patrol the slopes. He had laughed off my worries about too many other skilled candidates.

"Either the ski school or the resort will hire me, Jake. You'll see." His dimple had shown then; there must be something he hadn't told me yet.

But that was okay, there would be time. A lifetime, I hoped, although first there was the small matter of what Kurt would do while I spent four years in Denver. "That will work out too,

Jake," he'd said, one second before shucking me out of my utility pants.

He'd been right about everything else; I'd trust him on this. I trusted him with my life, and now I was entrusting him with my heart. I hadn't come right out and said that I loved him, but —I think Kurt knew.

ABOUT THE AUTHOR

P.D. Singer lives in Colorado with her slightly bemused husband, one proto-adult, and twelve pounds of cats. She's a big believer in research, firsthand if possible, so the reader can be quite certain Pam has skied down a mountain face first, been stepped on by rodeo horses, acquired a potato burn or two, and will never, ever, write a novel that includes skydiving.

When not writing, playing her fiddle, or skiing, she can be found with a book in hand.

Follow the adventures at Pam's website.

Keep current with Pam and the Rocky Ridge gang by joining the newsletter.

ALSO BY P.D. SINGER

Snow on the Mountain

Fall Down the Mountain

Blood on the Mountain

Return to the Mountain

Running to Him

Spokes

The Rare Event

A New Man

Diving Deep

Concierge Service

A TASTE OF SNOW ON THE MOUNTAIN
CHAPTER 1 (A KURT AND JAKE NOVEL)

The screams snapped my attention uphill. Nothing should have been happening behind my back. The skiers were supposed to sit still and let the chairlift take them to the top of the bunny slope. Quiet, other than the thrum of the machinery and the occasional conversation, was more usual. I was loading a munchkin-age ski class—they were wide-eyed and quieter than I expected. I'd slowed the lift to about half speed to seat them, which may have been all that saved that child.

A little girl shrieked and a second voice joined in, then more. "Do nothing fast" was really important now as I further slowed and then stopped the lift. Any quick motions would dislodge the small boy who now dangled upside down by one ski caught in the chairlift.

I knew how easily those bindings would release—I came out of mine every time I fell. A twist of an ankle would bring the child plummeting to the snow twenty feet below. His panicked thrashings made that more likely with every passing second.

"Jake, I call ski patrol!" yelled Egon, groping for the radio with his gloved hand. I hoped his accent wouldn't thicken beyond understanding from the tension, but he was already in the control hut and knew the channels. Have to learn those, but not in the middle of an emergency.

"Then come and help me!" I yelled back. I dashed into and out of the hut where Egon had been keeping watch. He barely noticed me scooping up the climbing rope and harness that he'd scolded me for even touching just a few days ago. The ski patrol did the rescues, he'd informed me snottily; the lowly lift operators were not to handle the equipment. I'd ignored him.

This kid couldn't wait for the patrol to show. Every second he stayed up was a gift from the heavens—he didn't have the minutes to spare for the experts. "Don't wiggle, kid! Hold real still! I'm coming up to get you!" I kept yelling at him to stop thrashing as I unraveled the coils. His chair had come to a halt about seventy yards from the loading area. I ran up the hill, glad for the packed snow under the lift.

I flung the rope up and over the cable, fully expecting to get elbowed out of the way. Whoever went up to fetch would only get there that much faster if the rope was already installed. The kid's hat fell on me. The kid might be next. I slung the end with the ascenders into position, feeding line and letting the weight of the hardware pull the rope over the cable. The other end of the rope had knots every few feet and would have fouled on the cable, something I would not have known if I hadn't scrutinized the equipment against Egon's wishes.

"Hold still, kid, we're coming!" I could see his wide, panicked eyes staring straight down at the unforgiving snow, which would snap his neck just as surely as concrete if he came out of that ski binding. The screaming from his seat partner and the kids in other chairs hadn't abated, though he was quiet now. There was no sign of the patrol—surely they'd be here in an instant? Egon appeared beside me, angling to be under the child to break his fall.

Where was the patrol? I had both ends of the rope together, so I shoved them at Egon. "Hold this taut! Tight!" His English was good, but.... The harness was attached to one jumar, the clip that stayed in one place with weight on it but would slide when unweighted. Where was the patrol? The kid was starting to shriek again, so I thrust my legs into the harness and brought the loose end around my waist to clip myself in.

Kurt had taught me to do this, though neither of us had ever envisioned the novice climber being the one to attempt a rescue. But it was me or Egon, who wasn't moving, and I knew I could get up that rope fast. "Keep it real tight. I'm going up!" I snarled at him. I grasped the doubled rope with my feet braced against the knots and jumared my hands up the other side. Kurt had emphasized safety over speed, but this kid's safety lay in speed because he could come down at any time. I was clipped in, that was as safe as it was going to get. I'd come down hard, too, if Egon couldn't keep enough weight on the rope. Maybe someone was down there helping him by now, but I dared not spend the attention to look.

"Hang on! I'm almost there," I kept reassuring the little boy and myself. A few more feet and I'd reach the chair. Hauling upward with my arms and pushing up with my feet on the knots was getting me where I needed to go. Little hands reached to me once I made it the last foot to chair level—I snagged the boy. He nearly strangled me with his arms around my neck. "I won't let you fall. I promise."

I could promise that now; it hadn't been a certainty at all. "We're going to go up a little more, okay?" I had to, or I wouldn't be able to get him unhitched. That damned binding should have released him with all the torque we were putting on it, and it was stuck fast. I had no more hands available, so I hauled us up the rope with another few pulls of the jumars and clung for dear life with my feet, once I finally found one of the knots. He had U-turned as we went up and was upright again. I hoped he wouldn't pass out on me. "See, I got you," I crooned. I tried to decide how to get him untangled, now that the danger of a fall was past. At least he wasn't howling any more.

His ski was caught in the safety bar of the chair, but I had a second child to worry about while I fixed that. "Sweetie, you are going to sit real still while I lift the bar to get your friend unstuck, okay?" I tried to smile reassuringly at the little girl who had been uncorking the ear-splitting screeches. "All you have to do is sit real still." Suggesting that she might fall out if she didn't was a fast track to more screaming, I thought. She blinked at me and nodded a fraction of an inch. "Yeah, real still. Good, good…."

I felt like I was talking to one of the horses at the Rendezvous Lake Lodge stables, but the more I talked, the calmer she got, and the little guy who clung to me stayed still and quiet while I lifted the safety bar with one hand to release his ski. It swung around and finally came free, clipping me hard in the knee. The pain made me gasp, but I didn't drop anything or anyone. Now I wondered if I should take them both down. Where was the class instructor? They were wearing the number bibs of a ski school—more bibs were on the chairs ahead of us and on the one behind. The instructor was below me, apparently, along with a patrol, at last. I didn't want to get the kids, however frightened, separated from the rest of the group, but I wasn't the nanny on skis.

"Up or down?" I yelled.

"Up!" the instructor called back. "Go with them!" She

sprinted, or maybe clumped, back down to her skis, which she'd abandoned at the loading zone. "I'll meet you at the top!"

Of course I'd go with them. One screamer and one clinger would feel a whole lot better with an adult. No way was I was going to send two frightened children up the mountain alone.

"Looks like I get to ride with you guys!" I said with a brightness I didn't feel. "You sit down on this side, and I'll get in the middle." There would be just enough room if I didn't drop anyone getting in. The little boy let me put him in the lift chair and shifted his death grip from my neck to the chair arm. I was scared I'd tip the chair with my weight, but I was able to pull myself up one more arm's reach with the jumars and drop into the seat without altering the balance. The safety bar came down first, then I unclipped the harness from the rope. The kids seemed to approve of my priorities; they relaxed just a little, and the girl clutched the bar with her mittened hands.

"We're good!" I called down, and Egon, who had neither complained nor let go, began to haul the rope off the cable. He'd kept that rope taut, which must have taken his entire body weight, or the unanchored rope would have dropped me right out of midair.

"Wait for me at the top!" called the ski patrol, making my heart sink. I'd usurped his role in this rescue, certain that the child wouldn't remain dangling for long. I wondered how much trouble I was in.

That was going to have to wait while I chatted with my new buddies. By the time we got to the top of the mountain, they should be over the worst of their fright. I didn't want this event to spoil their perceptions of skiing, the way a broken ankle had spoiled mine.

The ride to the top let the kids relax; the little girl decided I was a good guy and snuggled up against me on the one side, and the little boy, cause of all this, wanted my arm over his shoulders. It was cold enough that I put my hat on him and hoped that the instructor had grabbed the one that had fallen on me. The lift started to move again, so I started asking questions, which got one-word answers at first. Soon they were yakking away as if nothing had ever happened, telling me their names, Gracie and Todd, that they were twins, five years old, almost six, and that they loved skiing more than anything.

We had a short way to the top when I asked the vital question. "Todd, what were you doing when you fell out?"

"See the pretties?" He pointed at the trees to either side of the lifts—people had thrown Mardi Gras necklaces into the branches. The trees were festooned in bright beads: purple, green, silver, gold. "Mama likes pretties, so I tried to get one for her. But they were too far away, and I fell out."

A child had nearly died for some festive trash. Such beads were common, Kurt told me when I'd asked, and I'd only thought it amusing. Now I wondered how many times I'd be shimmying up a rope, and if the child would end up clutching my waist or broken in the snow.

"They're too far away. I couldn't reach, and I've got grownup arms." I waved my arm out the side of the chair to demonstrate. "Promise you won't grab at them again?"

"Okay," he agreed with a mutinous pout. "But there was a close one."

"Not that close," I reminded him. He grinned at me, and I quit worrying about Todd no longer enjoying skiing and began to wonder more about what else he'd find to get into.

"Your job as a skier is to sit quietly on the chair until it's time to get off," I told them. "Which is now." I lifted the bar and helped them offload, help they probably didn't need, I thought enviously as they skied over to the little group of bibs who had already reached the top. They probably skied as well as I did; they could afford to be fearless because they didn't have nearly so far to fall. The instructor was a few chairs behind us, so I waited with the little group, none much bigger than my pals and none with ski poles.

Todd was done with me, but Gracie held my hand and chattered at the children, and when the instructor got to the top with the last of the kids, she introduced me.

"Miss Julie, this is Jake, he saved Todd, he's so cool!" All of this was getting recorded for posterity—I noticed a few people with their cell phones out taking pictures. Maybe videos. I didn't want to think about how many times my face would be on YouTube by tonight. One of the picture takers fell into a snow bank, and I couldn't bring myself to feel sorry for him.

Miss Julie checked Todd over carefully, though he was all agog to get back down the mountain and tried to squirm away. I checked out Julie: about my age, brunette curls exploding at the ends of long braids and a figure that looked all right even in insulated pants. Kurt had said the resort wanted good-looking employees. She looked like confirmation of his statement. If she always got the very young students, I was going to be seeing her a lot at the bunny slope lift.

"I guess he's okay. He's acting like his usual daredevil self," she said, swapping his blue hat with the big white pom-pom for my gray beanie. I was glad to get my head covered again, since my ears might freeze solid in another five minutes.

"I asked him if anything hurt, and he said no. More shaken than anything, and even that didn't last." I had to smile—Todd was scooting down the slope two feet at a time. He'd be at the foot of the mountain before this conversation was done if we didn't hurry. "He wanted to grab one of the necklaces in the trees for his mother."

"Figures," she said darkly. "His mother knows all about getting men to give her jewelry." I raised my eyebrows at her, and she squinched her face with embarrassment. "Did I say that out loud? Forget I said that, please." Her eyes carried a hint of flirtation.

Wondering who Todd's mother was, I just said, "Don't worry."

The ski patrol had off-loaded and had joined us. "Is the kid okay?" he asked Julie.

"The kid trying hardest to get away is the one who was upside down. He's fine, Mark." She spoke into her radio, and then she and her little crew were off to shouts of "Pizza slice turns! Follow me!" The line of tiny skiers, even Todd, trailed her across the snow doing snowplow turns, though Gracie had to hug me one last time before she followed the class, skiing with skill that none matched, except Todd.

The ski patrol introduced himself as Mark McAvoy and asked all the details of the rescue before he got to the question that worried me. "Why didn't you wait?" There was no anger in the question, making me think he only wanted to know, not that he wanted to admonish me.

"I knew how to use the equipment, and I thought the kid's ski was going to come off any second. It was about twenty feet down. I figured that I'd have the rope up for you, and then it didn't seem safe to wait any more."

"I'm glad you didn't, even if the lift operators aren't supposed to do that sort of thing. He could have come down at any minute. You were most of the way up the rope before I got there. I was halfway down the Galloping Goose; it took me a couple of minutes." That was an intermediate run, marked with a blue square on the maps, which led into the bunny hill.

I laughed, more at the name of the run than anything else.

This mountain had trails named everything from Helium Heights to Fast Track to Nowhere. The names at least told you exactly where you were, and it was a lot more fun to say "I fell twice on The Cereal Bowl," than "I fell twice on Easy Number Three."

"I figured you'd say something if I needed to know."

"I wasn't about to joggle your elbow, although you could have clipped the kid in with that extra webbing on the harness instead of your arm, but he was thin enough you could reach around him. You do some rock climbing?" Mark sounded friendly.

"Some. I've used jumars. Ascenders." Wish I'd realized about that extra strap; it might have saved me some worry.

"Good thing too." He made some notes in a pocket-sized notebook. "What's your full name? I'll need to put it in the report."

"Landon. Jake Landon."

"That's your alias today, Mr. Bond?" He smiled warmly, but I was rather proud of myself for performing some derring-do.

"I think I've got all the details, but what's your number if I need anything more?" He wrote it down and stuck the notebook into his pocket. "I'll see you round. There's a little pub that caters to the ski workers, not the tourists. Some of us get a beer there now and then. I could give you a call." He quirked an eyebrow, which disappeared into his hat.

"Thanks. I'm not much of a drinker, though." If the invitation was just friendly, and it included Kurt, then it might be nice to socialize with a group. We'd been hanging around home a lot since we'd come to Wapiti Creek because we weren't entirely clear on how to handle ourselves in public. Did we introduce each other as partners, roommates, friends? How out did we want to be?

Mark waved and skied down the hill, making it look like the easiest thing in the world. I headed back to the off-loading ramp and sat in a freshly emptied chair to get whirled around the big pulley and toted back down the hillside. On the way down, I considered the casual way Mark had basically asked me out. I wasn't used to that, by a long shot. He was as tall as I was and a lot more athletic, certainly more socially poised. Kind of good-looking, with brown hair long enough to escape his wool hat, and wide, sensuous lips. But he wasn't Kurt, so I didn't want anything more from him than some friendship.

On the trip down, I wondered if Kurt was worried about me looking elsewhere.

Read the rest.